Praise for
Bharati Mukherjee's most recent novel,
JASMINE

"A beautiful novel, poetic, exotic, perfectly controlled."

San Francisco Chronicle

"[A] rich novel . . . JASMINE stands as one of the most suggestive novels we have about what it is to become an American."

The New York Times Book Review

"Artful and arresting . . . Breathtaking."

Los Angeles Times Book Review

"Engrossing . . . Mukherjee once again presents all the shock, pain and liberation of exile and transformation. . . . With the uncanny third eye of the artist, Mukherjee forces us to see our country anew."

USA Today

Also by Bharati Mukherjee
Published by Fawcett Books:

WIFE
JASMINE
THE MIDDLEMAN AND OTHER STORIES

DARKNESS

Bharati Mukherjee

FAWCETT CREST · NEW YORK

A Fawcett Crest Book
Published by Ballantine Books
Copyright © 1985 by Bharati Mukherjee

ISBN 0-449-22099-0

Manufactured in the United States of America

First Ballantine Books Edition: May 1992

For Bernard Malamud

"Not that the story need be long, but it will take a long while to make it short."
—Henry David Thoreau

Acknowledgements

"Angela" first appeared in *Mother Jones*

"The Lady from Lucknow" first appeared in *Missouri Review*

"The World According to Hsü" first appeared in *Chatelaine*

"Isolated Incidents" first appeared in *Saturday Night*

"Tamurlane" first appeared in *The Canadian Forum*

"Saints" first appeared in *Three Penny Review*

Contents

Introduction

Most of these stories were written in a three-month burst of energy in the spring of 1984, in Atlanta, Georgia, while I was writer-in-residence at Emory University. "The World According to Hsü," "Isolated Incidents," "Courtly Vision" and "Hindus" were written a little earlier, in Montreal and Toronto.

That energy interests me now.

For a writer, energy is aggression; urgency colliding with confidence. Suddenly, everything is possible. Excluded worlds are opened, secretive characters reveal themselves. The writing-self is somehow united with the universe.

Until Atlanta—and it could have been anywhere in America—I had thought of myself, in spite of a white husband and two assimilated sons, as an expatriate. In my fiction, and in my Canadian experience, "immigrants" were lost souls, put upon and pathetic. Expatriates, on the other hand, knew all too well who and what they were, and what foul fate had befallen them.

Like V.S. Naipaul, in whom I imagined a model, I tried to explore state-of-the-art expatriation. Like Naipaul, I used a mordant and self-protective irony in describing my characters' pain. Irony promised both detachment from, and superiority over, those well-bred post-colonials much like myself, adrift in the new world, wondering if they would ever belong.

If you have to wonder, if you keep looking for signs, if you wait—surrendering little bits of a reluctant self every year, clutching the souvenirs of an ever-retreating past—you'll never belong, anywhere.

In the years that I spent in Canada—1966 to 1980—I discovered that the country is hostile to its citizens who had been born in hot, moist continents like Asia; that the country proudly boasts of its opposition to the whole concept of cultural assimilation. In the Indian immigrant community I saw a family of shared grievances. The purely "Canadian" stories in this collection were difficult to write and even more painful to live through. They are uneasy stories about expatriation.

The transformation as writer, and as resident of the new world, occurred with the act of immigration to the United States. Suddenly I was no longer aggrieved, except as a habit of mind. I had moved from being a "visible minority," against whom the nation had officially incited its less-visible citizens to react, to being just another immigrant. If I may put it in its harshest terms, it would be this: in Canada, I was frequently taken for a prostitute or shoplifter, frequently assumed to be a domestic, praised by astonished auditors that I didn't have a "sing-song" accent. The society itself, or important elements in that society, routinely made crippling assumptions about me, and about my "kind." In the United States, however, I see *myself* in those same outcasts; I see myself in an article on a Trinidad-Indian hooker; I see myself in the successful executive who slides Hindi film music in his tape deck as he drives into Manhattan; I see myself in the shady accountant who's trying to marry off his loose-living daughter; in professors, domestics, high school students, illegal busboys in ethnic restaurants. It's possible—with sharp ears and the right equipment—to hear America singing even in the seams of the dominant culture. In fact, it may be the best listening post for the next generation of Whitmans. For me, it is a movement away from the aloofness of expatriation, to the exuberance of immigration.

I have joined imaginative forces with an anonymous, driven, underclass of semi-assimilated Indians with sentimental attachments to a distant homeland but no real desire for permanent return. I see my "immigrant" story replicated in a dozen American cities, and instead of seeing my Indianness as a fragile identity to be preserved against obliteration (or worse, a "visible" disfigurement to be hidden), I see it now as a set of fluid identities to be celebrated. I see myself as an American writer in the tradition of other American writers whose parents or grandparents had passed through Ellis Island. Indianness is now a metaphor, a particular way of partially comprehending the world. Though the characters in these stories are, or were, "Indian," I see most of these as stories of broken identities and discarded languages, and the will to bond oneself to a new community, against the ever-present fear of failure and betrayal. The book I dream of updating is no longer *A Passage to India*—it's *Call It Sleep*.

Bernard Malamud, to whom this book is dedicated, is a man I have known for over twenty years as a close friend, but Bernard Malamud the writer is a man I have known only for these past two years, after I learned to read his stories as part of the same celebration.

Angela

ORRIN and I are in Delia's hospital room. There's no place to sit because we've thrown our parkas, caps and scarves on the only chair. The sides of Delia's bed have metal railings so we can't sit on her bed as we did on Edith's when Edith was here to have her baby last November. The baby, if a girl, was supposed to be named Darlene after Mother, but Edith changed her mind at the last minute. She changed her mind while she was being shaved by the nurse. She picked "Ramona" out of a novel.

My sisters are hopeless romantics.

Orrin loves Delia and brings her little gifts. Yesterday he brought her potted red flowers from Hy-Vee and jangly Mexican earrings I can't quite see Delia wearing; the day before he tied a pair of big, puffy dice to the bedrails. Today he's carrying *One Hundred Years of Solitude.* Delia can't read. She's in a coma, but any day she might come out of it.

He's so innocent! I want to hold his head in my hands, I want to stop up his ears with my fingers so he can't hear Dr. Menezies speak. The doctor is a heavy, gloomy man from Goa, India. Hard work got him where he is. He dismisses Orrin's optimism as frivolous and childish.

"We could read twenty or thirty pages a day to her." Orrin pokes me through my sweater. "You want to start reading?" It's a family joke that I hate to read my English isn't good enough yet—and Orrin's almost family. "It's like 'Dynasty,' only more weird."

"You read. I'll get us some coffee."

"A Diet Coke for me."

Dr. Vinny Menezies lies in wait for me by the vending machines. "Hullo, hullo." He jerks his body into bows as I get myself coffee. "You brighten my day." He's an old-fashioned suitor, an unmarried immigrant nearing forty. He has put himself through medical school in Bombay and Edinburgh, and now he's ready to take a wife, preferably a younger woman who's both affectionate and needy. We come from the same subcontinent of hunger and misery: that's a bonus, he told me.

I feel in the pockets of my blue jeans for quarters, and the coffee slops out of a paper cup.

"I'm making you nervous, Angie?" Dr. Menezies extracts a large, crisp handkerchief from his doctor's white jacket, and blots my burning fingertips. "You're so shy, so sensitive."

He pronounces the "s" in sensitive as a "z."

"Do you have a nickel for five pennies? I need to get a Coke for poor Orrin."

"Of course." He holds a shiny nickel out to me. He

strokes my palm as I count out the pennies. "That boy-friend of Delia's, he's quite mental with grief, no?"

"He loves her," I mumble.

"And I you."

But Dr. Menezies lightens the gravity of his confession by choosing that moment to kick the stuck candy machine.

A week before the accident Orrin asked Delia to marry him. Delia told me this. I've been her sister for less than two years, but we tell each other things. Bad and good. I told her about the cook at the orphanage, how he'd chop wings off crows with his cleaver so I could sew myself a sturdy pair of angel wings. He said I was as good as an angel and the wings would be my guarantee. He'd sit me on the kitchen floor and feed me curried mutton and rice, creamy custards meant for Bishop Pymm. Delia told me about her black moods. Nobody knows about the black moods; they don't show, she's always so sweet tempered. She's afraid she's going crazy. Most of the time she loves Orrin, but she doesn't want him to marry a nut.

Orrin calls me by name, his special name for me. "Angel," he says. "Tell me, was she going to say yes?"

I pull open the flip-top of his Diet Coke. He needs looking after, especially now.

"You've come to know her better than any of us." He sits on the windowsill, his feet on the chair. His shoes squash our winter things. "Please, I can handle the truth."

"Of course, she loves you, Orrin." In the dry heat

of Delia's hospital room, even my smile is charged with static.

Delia's eyes are open. We can't tell what she sees or hears. It would have been easier on us if she'd looked as though she were sleeping. Orrin chats to her and holds her hand. He makes plans. He'll quit his job with the Presbyterian Youth Outreach Council. He'll move back from Des Moines. When Delia gets out, they'll fly to Nicaragua and work on a farm side by side with Sandinistas. Orrin's an idealist.

I believe in miracles, not chivalry.

Grace makes my life spin. How else does a girl left for dead in Dakha get to the Brandons' farmhouse in Van Buren County?

When I was six, soldiers with bayonets cut off my nipples. "They left you poor babies for dead," Sister Stella at the orphanage would tell me, the way I might tell Ramona bedtime stories. "They left you for dead, but the Lord saved you. Now it's your turn to do Him credit."

We are girls with special missions. Some day soon, the mysteries will be revealed. When Sister Stella was my age, she was a Muslim, the daughter of a man who owned jute mills. Then she fell in love with a tourist from Marseilles, and when he went home she saw him for what he was: the Lord's instrument for calling her to Christianity. Reading portents requires a special kind of literacy.

Mrs. Grimlund, the nurse, steals into the room in her laced, rubber-soled shoes. Dr. Menezies is with her. "Hullo, again." At the end of a long afternoon, his white doctor's jacket looks limp, but his voice is eager.

"Don't look so glum. Delia isn't dying." He doesn't actually ignore Orrin, but it's me he wants to talk to.

Orrin backs off to the window. "We aren't looking glum," he mutters.

Dr. Menezies fusses with Delia's chart. "We're giving her our best. Not to worry, please."

Mrs. Grimlund, deferential, helps out Dr. Menezies. "My, my," she says in a loud, throaty voice, "we're looking a lot livelier today, aren't we?" She turns her blue, watchful eyes on Orrin. As a nurse and a good Christian she wants to irradiate the room with positive thinking. She marches to the window and straightens a bent shutter. Then she eases the empty Coke can out of Orrin's hand and drops it in the wastebasket. She can always find things that need doing. When I first got to Iowa, she taught me to skate on the frozen lake behind our church.

Dr. Menezies plucks Delia's left hand out from under the blanket and times her pulse. His watch is flat, a gold wafer on a thick, hairy wrist. It looks expensive. His silk tie, the band of shirt that shows between the lapels of his jacket, even the fountain pen with gold clip, look very expensive. He's a spender. Last Christmas he gave me a choker of freshwater pearls he'd sent for from Macy's catalog.

"Splendid," he agrees. But it's me he's looking at. "Very satisfactory indeed." In spite of my bony, scarred body and plain face.

Sometimes I visualize grace as a black, tropical bat, cutting through dusk on blunt, ugly wings.

"You wonder why a thing like this happens," Mrs. Grimlund whispers. She lacks only imagination. She tucks Delia's hand back under the blanket and tidies up

Orrin's gifts on the night table. I brought a bag of apples. For Orrin, not Delia. Someone has to make him keep up his energies. "She's such a sweet, loving Christian person."

Orrin turns on her. "Don't look for the hand of Providence in this! It was an accident. Delia hit an icy patch and lost control of the wheel." He twists and twists the shutter control.

"Let me get you another Coke," I beg.

"Stop mothering me!"

Orrin needs to move around. He walks from the window to the bed, where Dr. Menezies is holding his flashlight like a lorgnette, then back to the window. He sits on the chair, on top of our parkas. I hate to see him this lost.

"Delia always carries her witness," Mrs. Grimlund goes on. "I never once saw her upset or angry." She's known Delia all of Delia's life. She told me that it was Delia who asked specifically for a sister from Bangladesh. She was dropping me off after choir practice last week and she said, "Delia said, 'I have everything, so I want a sister who has nothing. I want a sister I can really share my things with.'"

I never once saw her angry either. I did see her upset. The moods came on her very suddenly. She'd read the papers, a story about bad stuff in a day-care center maybe, about little kids being fondled and photographed, then she'd begin to cry. The world's sins weighed on her.

Orrin can't seem to stay in the chair. He stumbles toward the door. He isn't trying to leave Delia's room, he's just trying to get hold of himself.

Once Orrin goes out of the room, Mrs. Grimlund lets

go a little of her professional cheeriness. "It just pulls the rug from under you, doesn't it? You wonder why?"

I was in the backseat, that's how I got off with a stiff neck. I have been blessed. The Lord keeps saving me.

Delia was driving and little Kim was in the bucket seat, telling a funny story on Miss Wendt, his homeroom teacher. Mother says that when Kim first got here, he didn't speak a word of anything, not even Korean. He was four. She had to teach him to eat lunch slowly. Kim was afraid the kids at school might snatch it if he didn't eat real fast.

He braced himself when we went into that spin. He broke his wrist and sprained his ankle, and the attendant said probably nothing would have happened if he'd just relaxed and sort of collapsed, when he saw it coming.

"There's no telling, is there?" The world's mysteries have ravaged Mrs. Grimlund. Her cap has slipped slightly off-center. "Who'll be taken and who'll be saved, I mean."

Dr. Menezies gives her a long, stern look. "Our job is not to wonder, but to help." He reaches across Delia to touch my arm.

Mrs. Grimlund reddens. What was meant as rebuke comes off as a brisk, passionate outburst. The dingy thicknesses of coat and shirt envelop a wild, raw heart. In the hospital he seems a man of circumspect feelings, but on Sunday afternoons when we drive around and around in his Scirocco, his manner changes. He seems raw, aimless, lost.

"I didn't mean anything wicked," Mrs. Grimlund whispers. "I wasn't questioning the Lord's ways."

I calm her with my smile. My winning smile, that's what the Brandons call it. "Of course you didn't." I am Angela the Angel. Angela was Sister Stella's name for me. The name I was born with is lost to me, the past is lost to me. I must have seen a lot of wickedness when I was six, but I can't remember any of it. The rapes, the dogs chewing on dead bodies, the soldiers. Nothing.

Orrin rushes in from the hall. Dr. Menezies, his passion ebbed, guides Orrin to the chair and I grab the parkas so Orrin will have more room to sit. He needs looking after. I imagine him among Sandinista farmers. He tells slight, swarthy men carrying machetes about rootworms and cutworms. His eyes develop a savior's glittery stare.

"We shouldn't be just standing around and chattering," he shouts. "We're chattering in front of her as though she's dead."

He's all wired up with grief. He was up most of last night, but he doesn't look tired. He looks angry, crazy, stunned, but not tired. He can be with Delia two more days, then he has to go back to Des Moines.

"Take him home." Dr. Menezies is at his best now. He takes charge. He helps Orrin into his jacket and hands him his scarf, cap, mittens. "He isn't doing Delia any good in this state. We have our hands full as it is."

Mrs. Grimlund watches me pull a glove on with my teeth. "I didn't mean it should have been you, Angie." Her lower lip's chewed so deep that there's blood.

Then Dr. Menezies' heavy arm rests on my shoulder. If his watch were any closer to my ear, I'd hear it hum. "Give my regards to your dear parents," he says. He makes a courtly, comical bow. "I shall be seeing you on Sunday? Yes, please?"

On Sunday, after church, we sit down to a huge pork roast—pigs aren't filthy creatures here as they are back home—and applesauce, mashed potatoes and gravy, candied carrots, hot rolls. My older sister Edith, and Mary Wellman, the widow from two farms over, have brought dessert: two fruit pies, a chocolate cake and a small jar of macaroons. My brother Bill's wife, Judy, is studying for her Master's in Library Science, so she usually brings something simple, like tossed salad.

I love these Sunday dinners. Company isn't formal and wearying as it was in the orphanage. The days that the trustees in their silk saris and high heels sat at our tables were headachy and endless. The Brandons talk about everything: what Reverend Gertz said about Salvadoran refugees, the blizzard we've just gone through, the tardy Farm Bureau officials who still haven't authorized the loan for this season's plantings. Dad's afraid that if the money doesn't come through by the end of March, he and a whole lot of farmers in the county will be in trouble.

"It'll come through." Mother's the Rock of Gibraltar in our house. She forks carrot slivers delicately and leans her head a wee bit toward Judy who is telling us about her first husband. "I wouldn't let him near the children, I don't care what the judge says." Bill just melts away from conversations about Judy's first husband. Mother wanted to be a school teacher, Delia told me. She wanted to help kids with learning difficulties. Delia wants to be a physical therapist.

"I shouldn't be so sanguine," Ron says. Ron is Edith's husband. He worked for John Deere until the big lay-off, but he's not waiting for recall. He's training himself for computers at the Community College, and during the day he sits in a cubicle in a hall full of cubicles and makes phone calls for a mail-order firm. The firm sells diet pills and offers promotional gifts. Ron thinks the whole thing's a scam to misuse credit cards.

"Oh, you always look on the negative side," Edith scolds. She eats at the small table—to the left of the dining table—with Kim and Fred and Ramona. Fred is Judy's six-year-old. She's expecting a baby with Bill in the spring. Ramona is propped up and strapped into her white plastic feeding seat. Edith lifts teaspoonsful of mashed potatoes to Ramona's full, baby lips. "She really goes for your gravy, Mom. Don't you, darling?"

Ron reaches into the basket of rolls. "Well, life hasn't been too upscale lately for any of us!"

Dr. Menezies bobs and weaves in his chair, passing the plate of butter curls and the gravy boat. He's clearly the most educated, the most travelled man at the table, but he talks the least. He is polite, too polite, passing platters and tureens, anticipating and satisfying. This Sunday his hair springs in two big, glossy waves from a thin parting, and his mustache has a neat droop. He tries to catch my eye as he passes the butter.

"I don't know what we'd have done without you, Vinny," Dad says. Dad looks away at the yard, and beyond it at the fields that may not get planted this season.

We have deep feelings, but we aren't a demonstrative

family. Fellowship is what we aim for. A parent's griev-
ing would be a spectacle in Bangladesh.

Dr. Menezies tugs at his mustache. It could be a
pompous gesture, but somehow he manages to make it
seem gracious. "It was my duty only, sir."

I can tell he is thrilled with Dad's praise.

Around three-thirty, after Edith and her family and
Bill and his family have driven away, and Mary Wellman, Mother and I have washed and dried the dishes,
I play Mozart on the piano for Dr. Menezies. He likes
to watch me play, he says. He's tone-deaf, but he says
he likes the way the nuns taught me to sit, straight
and elegant, on the piano bench. A little civility is
how he thinks of this Sunday afternoon ritual. It's one
more civility that makes the immense, snowy Mid-
west less alarming, less ambiguous. I throw myself
into the "Fantasy in C Minor," the "Exultation."
The music, gliding on scarred fingers, transports me
to the assembly hall of the orphanage. The Bishop
sits in the front row, flanked by the trustees in their
flowered saris, and a row or two behind, blissful Sister Stella, my teacher. The air in the hall is sweet and
lustrous. Together, pianist and audience, we have tri-
umphed over sin, rapacity, war, all that's shameful in
human nature.

"Bravo!" the doctor shouts, forgetting himself, forgetting we're in a farmhouse parlor in the middle of
America, only Mary Wellman, my parents, and himself
to listen. He claps his soft fists, and his gold watch
reflects, a pure white flame, on a window pane. "Bravo,
bravo!"

When I've lowered the lid, Mary Wellman gathers up

her coat and cake pan. I've wrapped what was left of the chocolate cake in tinfoil and she carries the small, shiny package breast-high as if it is a treasure. Then Mother excuses herself and goes up to her room to crochet an afghan for Christmas. She doesn't know whom she's making it for, yet. She knits, she crochets. On Sundays, she doesn't read, not even the Des Moines *Register*.

Dad joins Kim in the basement for basketball. Dr. Menezies doesn't care for basketball. Or football or baseball. He came to America as a professional, too old to pick up on some things. The trivia, the madness, elude him. He approaches the New World with his stethoscope drawn; he listens to its scary gurgles. He leaves the frolicking to natives. Kim and I are forced to assimilate. A girl with braids who used to race through wet, leechy paddy-fields now skates on frozen water: that surely is a marvel. And the marvels replicate. The coach has put me on the varsity cheerleading squad. To make me feel wanted. I'm grateful. I am wanted. Love is waving big, fluffy pom-poms in school colors; it's wearing new Nikes and leaping into the air. I'd never owned shoes in Bangladesh. All last winter, when Delia played—they said she was tough on the boards, she was intimidating, awesome, second team All-State, from a school of only two hundred—I shook my pom-poms fiercely from the court's edge, I screamed my sisterly love. Delia sent for me from Dakha. She knew what her special mission was when she was just in tenth grade. I could die not knowing, not being able even to guess.

"We're alone. At last."

                              * * *

Dr. Menezies floats toward me on squeaky new leather shoes. He's the acquisitor. His voice is hoarse, but his face is radiant. He should not alarm me now. After three-thirty on Sunday afternoons, the Brandons leave the front room to us, and nothing untoward ever happens.

I retreat to the upright piano. Shockingly, my body trembles. "Where did everyone go? We seem to be the only idle ones around here."

The doctor laughs. "Idleness is the devil's workshop, no?"

I suggest a walk. But my suitor does not want to walk or go for a drive. He wants to sit beside me on the piano bench and whimper from the fullness of love.

I hold my shoulders pressed back, my spine taut and straight, so straight, the way Sister Stella taught me. Civilities to see us through minor crises.

"You must be worrying all the time about your future, no?" He strokes my hair, my neck. His inflection is ardent. "Your school will be over in May."

"In June."

"May, June, okay. But then what?" He rubs the lumpy scars between my shoulder blades.

There's a new embarrassing twitchiness to my body. My thighs, squeezed tight, begin to hurt.

"In America, grown-up children are expected to fly the coop," my suitor explains. "You will have to fly, Angie. Make your own life. No shilly-shally, no depending on other people here."

"I thought I'd go to Iowa City. Study physical therapy, like Delia."

"Delia will never study physical therapy, Angie."

His voice is deep, but quiet, though we are alone. "You are the strong one. I can tell you."

Mrs. Grimlund dances a sad, savage dance on weightless feet. There's no telling who'll be taken and who'll be saved. I wait for some sign. I've been saved for a purpose.

"Anyway, you're going to make the Brandons shell out three-four thousand dollars? I don't think you're so selfish." He gives a shy giggle, but his face is intense. "I think when school is over, you'll be wanting to find a full-time job. Yes. You'll want to find a job. Or a husband. If it is the latter, I'm a candidate putting in an early word."

He slips a trembling arm around my waist and pulls me close. A wet, shy kiss falls like a blow on the side of my head.

Tomorrow when I visit Delia, I'll stop by the Personnel Department. They know me, my family. I'll work well with handicapped children. With burn-center children. I'll not waste my life.

But that night, in the room with two beds, Dr. Menezies lies on Delia's pink chenille bedspread. His dark, ghostly face rests on pillowshams trimmed with pink lace. He offers me intimacy, fellowship. He tempts with domesticity. Phantom duplexes, babies tucked tight into cribs, dogs running playfully off with the barbecued steak.

What am I to do?

Only a doctor could love this body.

Then it is the lavender dusk of tropics. Delinquents and destitutes rush me. Legless kids try to squirm out of ditches. Packs of pariah dogs who have learned to gorge on dying infant flesh, soldiers with silvery bayonets, they keep coming at me, plunging their knives through my arms and shoulders. I dig my face into the muddy walls of a trough too steep to climb. Leeches, I can feel leeches gorging on the blood of my breasts.

The Lady
from Lucknow

WHEN I was four, one of the girls next door fell in love with a Hindu. Her father intercepted a love note from the boy, and beat her with his leather sandals. She died soon after. I was in the room when my mother said to our neighbor, "The Nawab-*sahib* had no choice, but Husseina's heart just broke, poor dear." I was an army doctor's daughter, and I pictured the dead girl's heart—a rubbery squeezable organ with auricles and ventricles—first swelling, then bursting and coating the floor with thick, slippery blood.

We lived in Lucknow at the time, where the Muslim community was large. This was just before the British took the fat, diamond-shaped subcontinent and created two nations, a big one for the Hindus and a littler one for us. My father moved us to Rawalpindi in Pakistan two months after Husseina died. We were a family of soft, voluptuous children, and my father wanted to protect us from the Hindus' shameful lust.

I have fancied myself in love many times since, but

16

never enough for the emotions to break through tissue and muscle. Husseina's torn heart remains the standard of perfect love.

At seventeen I married a good man, the fourth son of a famous poet-cum-lawyer in Islamabad. We have a daughter, seven, and a son, four. In the Muslim communities we have lived in, we are admired. Iqbal works for IBM, and because of his work we have made homes in Lebanon, Brazil, Zambia and France. Now we live in Atlanta, Georgia, in a wide, new house with a deck and a backyard that runs into a golf course. IBM has been generous to us. We expect to pass on this good, decent life to our children. Our children are ashamed of the dingy cities where we got our start.

Some Sunday afternoons when Iqbal isn't at a conference halfway across the world, we sit together on the deck and drink gin and tonics as we have done on Sunday afternoons in a dozen exotic cities. But here, the light is different somehow. A gold haze comes off the golf course and settles on our bodies, our new house. When the light shines right in my eyes, I pull myself out of the canvas deck chair and lean against the railing that still smells of forests. Everything in Atlanta is so new!

"Sit," Iqbal tells me. "You'll distract the golfers. Americans are crazy for sex, you know that."

He half rises out of his deck chair. He lunges for my breasts in mock passion. I slip out of his reach.

At the bottom of the backyard, the golfers, caddies and carts are too minute to be bloated with lust.

But, who knows? One false thwock! of their golfing irons, and my little heart, like a golf ball, could slice through the warm air and vanish into the jonquil-yellow beyond.

* * *

It isn't trouble that I want, though I do have a lover. He's an older man, an immunologist with the Center for Disease Control right here in town. He comes to see me when Iqbal is away at high-tech conferences in sunny, remote resorts. Just think, Beirut was once such a resort! Lately my lover comes to me on Wednesdays even if Iqbal's in town.

"I don't expect to live till ninety-five," James teases on the phone. His father died at ninety-three in Savannah. "But I don't want a bullet in the brain from a jealous husband right now."

Iqbal owns no firearms. Jealousy would inflame him.

Besides, Iqbal would never come home in the middle of the day. Not even for his blood pressure pills. The two times he forgot them last month, I had to take the bottle downtown. One does not rise through the multinational hierarchy coming home in midday, arriving late, or leaving early. Especially, he says, if you're a "not-quite" as we are. It is up to us to set the standards.

Wives who want to be found out will be found out. Indiscretions are deliberate. The woman caught in mid-shame is a woman who wants to get out. The rest of us carry on.

James flatters me indefatigably; he makes me feel beautiful, exotic, responsive. I am a creature he has immunized of contamination. When he is with me, the world seems a happy enough place.

Then he leaves. He slips back into his tweed suit and backs out of my driveway.

I met James Beamish at a reception for foreign students on the Emory University campus. Iqbal avoids these international receptions because he thinks of them as excuses for looking back when we should be looking forward. These evenings are almost always tedious, but I like to go; just in case there's someone new and fascinating. The last two years, I've volunteered as host in the "hospitality program." At Thanksgiving and Christmas, two lonely foreign students are sent to our table.

That first evening at Emory we stood with name tags on lapels, white ones for students and blue ones for hosts. James was by a long table, pouring Chablis into a plastic glass. I noticed him right off. He was dressed much like the other resolute, decent men in the room. But whereas the other men wore white or blue shirts under their dark wool suits, James's shirt was bright red.

His wife was with him that evening, a stoutish woman with slender ankles and expensive shoes.

"Darling," she said to James. "See if you can locate our Palestinian." Then she turned to me, and smiling, peered into my name tag.

"I'm Nafeesa Hafeez," I helped out.

"Na-fee-sa," she read out. "Did I get that right?"

"Yes, perfect," I said.

"What a musical name," she said. "I hope you'll be very happy here. Is this your first time abroad?"

James came over with a glass of Chablis in each hand. "Did we draw this lovely lady? Oops, I'm sorry, you're a *host*, of course." A mocking blue light was in his eyes. "Just when I thought we were getting lucky, dear."

"Darling, ours is a Palestinian. I told you that in the car. This one is obviously not Palestinian, are you, dear?'' She took a bright orange notebook out of her purse and showed me a name.

I had to read it upside-down. Something Waheed. School of Dentistry.

"What are you drinking?" James asked. He kept a glass for himself and gave me the other one.

Maybe James Beamish said nothing fascinating that night, but he was attentive, even after the Beamishes' Palestinian joined us. Mrs. Beamish was brave, she asked the dentist about his family and hometown. The dentist described West Beirut in detail. The shortage of bread and vegetables, the mortar poundings, the babies bleeding. I wonder when aphasia sets in. When does a dentist, even a Palestinian dentist, decide it's time to cut losses.

Then my own foreign student arrived. She was an Indian Muslim from Lucknow, a large, bold woman who this far from our common hometown claimed me as a countrywoman. India, Pakistan, she said, not letting go of my hand, what does it matter?

I'd rather have listened to James Beamish but I couldn't shut out the woman's voice. She gave us her opinions on Thanksgiving rituals. She said, "It is very odd that the pumpkin vegetable should be used for dessert, no? We are using it as vegetable only. Chhi! Pumpkin as a sweet. The very idea is horrid."

I promised that when she came to our house for Thanksgiving, I'd make sweetmeats out of ricotta cheese and syrup. When you live in as many countries as Iqbal has made me, you can't tell if you pity, or if you envy, the women who stayed back.

* * *

I didn't hear from James Beamish for two weeks. I
thought about him. In fact I couldn't get him out of my
mind. I went over the phrases and gestures, the mocking light in the eyes, but they didn't add up to much.
After the first week, I called Amina and asked her to
lunch. I didn't know her well but her husband worked
at the Center for Disease Control. Just talking to someone connected with the Center made me feel good. I
slipped his name into the small talk with Amina and
her eyes popped open, "Oh, he's famous!" she exclaimed, and I shrugged modestly. I stayed home in
case he should call. I sat on the deck and in spite of the
cold, pretended to read Barbara Pym novels. Lines from
Donne and Urdu verses about love floated in my skull.

I wasn't sure Dr. Beamish would call me. Not directly,
that is. Perhaps he would play a subtler game, get his wife
to invite Iqbal and me for drinks. Maybe she'd even in-
clude their Palestinian and my Indian and make an international evening out of it. It sounded plausible.

Finally James Beamish called me on a Tuesday afternoon, around four. The children were in the kitchen,
and a batch of my special chocolate sludge cookies was
in the oven.

"Hi," he said, then nothing for a bit. Then he said,
"This is James Beamish from the CDC. I've been
thinking of you."

He was between meetings, he explained. Wednesday
was the only flexible day in his week, his day for paperwork. Could we have lunch on Wednesday?

The cookies smelled gooey hot, not burned. My
daughter had taken the cookie sheet out and put in a
new one. She'd turned the cold water faucet on so she

could let the water drip on a tiny rosebud burn on her arm.

I felt all the warm, familiar signs of lust and remorse. I dabbed the burn with an ice cube wrapped in paper towel and wondered if I'd have time to buy a new front-closing bra after Iqbal got home.

James and I had lunch in a Dekalb County motel lounge.

He would be sixty-five in July, but not retire till sixty-eight. Then he would live in Tonga, in Fiji, see the world, travel across Europe and North America in a Winnebago. He wouldn't be tied down. He had five daughters and two grandsons, the younger one aged four, a month older than my son. He had been in the navy during the war (*his* war), and he had liked that.

I said, " 'Goodbye, Mama, I'm off to Yokohama.' " It was silly, but it was the only war footage I could come up with, and it made him laugh.

"You're special," he said. He touched my knee under the table. "You've already been everywhere."

"Not because I've wanted to."

He squeezed my knee again, then paid with his MasterCard card.

As we were walking through the parking lot to his car (it was a Cougar or a Buick, and not German or British as I'd expected), James put his arm around my shoulders. I may have seen the world but I haven't gone through the American teenage rites of making out in parked cars and picnic grounds, so I walked briskly out of his embrace. He let his hand slide off my shoulder. The hand slid down my back. I counted three deft little pats to my bottom before he let his hand fall away.

Iqbal and I are sensual people, but secretive. The openness of James Beamish's advance surprised me.

I got in his car, wary, expectant.

"Do up the seatbelt," he said.

He leaned into his seatbelt and kissed me lightly on the lips. I kissed him back, hard. "You don't panic easily, do you?" he said. The mocking blue light was in his eyes again. His tongue made darting little thrusts and probes past my lips.

Yes, I do, I would have said if he'd let me.

We held hands on the drive to my house. In the driveway he parked behind my Honda. "Shall I come in?"

I said nothing. Love and freedom drop into our lives. When we have to beg or even agree, it's already too late.

"Let's go in." He said it very softly.

I didn't worry about the neighbors. In his gray wool slacks and tweed jacket, he looked too old, too respectable, for any sordid dalliance with a not-quite's wife.

Our house is not that different in size and shape from the ones on either side. Only the inside smells of heavy incense, and the walls are hung with rows of miniature paintings from the reign of Emperor Akbar. I took James's big wrinkled hand in mine. Adultery in my house is probably no different, no quieter, than in other houses in this neighborhood.

Afterwards it wasn't guilt I felt (guilt comes with desire not acted), but wonder that while I'd dashed out Tuesday night and bought myself silky new underwear, James Beamish had worn an old T-shirt and lemon-pale boxer shorts. Perhaps he hadn't planned on seducing a Lucknow lady that afternoon. Adventure and freedom had come to him out of the blue, too. Or perhaps only younger men like Iqbal make a fetish of doing sit-ups and dieting and renewing their membership at the racquet club when they're on the prowl.

October through February our passion held. When we were together, I felt cherished. I only played at being helpless, hysterical, cruel. When James left, I'd spend the rest of the afternoon with a Barbara Pym novel. I kept the novels open at pages in which excellent British women recite lines from Marvell to themselves. I didn't read. I watched the golfers trudging over brown fairways instead. I let the tiny golfers—clumsy mummers—tell me stories of ambitions unfulfilled. Golf carts lurched into the golden vista. I felt safe.

In the first week of March we met in James's house for a change. His wife was in Madison to babysit a grandson while his parents flew to China for a three-week tour. It was a thrill to be in his house. I fingered the book spines, checked the color of sheets and towels, the brand names of cereals and detergents. Jane Fonda's Workout record was on the VCR. He was a man who took exceptional care of himself, this immunologist. Real intimacy, at last. The lust of the winter months had been merely foreplay. I felt at home in his house, in spite of the albums of family photographs on the coffee table and the brutish metal vulvas sculpted by a daughter in art school and stashed in the den. James was more talkative in his own house. He showed me the photos he wanted me to see, named real lakes and mountains. His family was real, and not quite real. The daughters were hardy, outdoor types. I saw them hiking in Zermatt and bicycling through Europe. They had red cheeks and backpacks. Their faces were honest and

marvellously ordinary. What would they say if they
knew their father, at sixty-five, was in bed with a married woman from Lucknow? I feared and envied their
jealousy more than any violence in my husband's heart.

Love on the decline is hard to tell from love on the
rise. I have lived a life perched on the edge of ripeness
and decay. The traveller feels at home everywhere, because she is never at home anywhere. I felt the hot red
glow of blood rushing through capillaries.

His wife came back early, didn't call, caught a ride
from Hartsfield International with a friend. She had
been raised in Saskatchewan, and she'd remained thrifty.

We heard the car pull into the driveway, the loud
"thank yous" and "no, I couldn'ts" and then her surprised shout, "James? Are you ill? What're you doing
home?" as she shut the front door.

We were in bed, sluggishly cozy and still moist under
the goosedown quilt that the daughter in Madison had
sent them as a fortieth anniversary gift some years before. His clothes were on top of a long dresser; mine
were on the floor, the stockings wrinkled and looking
legless.

James didn't go to pieces. I had to admire that. He
said, "Get in the bathroom. Get dressed. I'll take care
of this."

I am submissive by training. To survive, the Asian
wife will usually do as she is told. But this time I stayed
in bed.

"How are you going to explain me away, James? Tell
her I'm the new cleaning woman?" I laughed, and my
laugh tinkled flirtatiously, at least to me.

"Get in the bathroom." This was the fiercest I'd ever heard him.

"I don't think so," I said. I jerked the quilt off my body but didn't move my legs.

So I was in bed with the quilt at my feet, and James was by the dresser buttoning his shirt when Kate Beamish stood at the door.

She didn't scream. She didn't leap for James's throat—or mine. I'd wanted passion, but Kate didn't come through. I pulled the quilt over me.

I tried insolence. "Is your wife not the jealous kind?" I asked.

"Let's just get over this as quietly and quickly as we can, shall we?" she said. She walked to the window in her brown Wallabies. "I don't see any unfamiliar cars, so I suppose you'll expect James to drive you home."

"She's the jealous type," James said. He moved toward his wife and tried to guide her out of the bedroom.

"I'm definitely the jealous kind," Kate Beamish said. "I might have stabbed you if I could take you seriously. But you are quite ludicrous lounging like a Goya nude on my bed." She gave a funny little snort. I noticed straggly hairs in her nostrils and looked away.

James was running water in the bathroom sink. Only the panicky ones fall apart and call their lawyers from the bedroom.

She sat on my side of the bed. She stared at me. If that stare had made me feel secretive and loathsome, I might not have wept, later. She plucked the quilt from my breasts as an internist might, and snorted again. "Yes," she said, "I don't deny a certain interest he might have had," but she looked through my face to the pillow behind, and dropped the quilt as she stood. I was a shadow without depth or color, a shadow-temptress who would float back to a city of teeming millions when the affair with James had ended.

I had thought myself provocative and fascinating. What had begun as an adventure had become shabby and complex. I was just another involvement of a white man in a pokey little outpost, something that "men do" and then come to their senses while the *memsahibs* drink gin and tonic and fan their faces. I didn't merit a stab wound through the heart.

It wasn't the end of the world. It was humorous, really. Still, I let James call me a cab. That half hour wait for the cab, as Kate related tales of the grandson to her distracted husband was the most painful. It came closest to what Husseina must have felt. At least her father, the Nawab-*sahib*, had beaten her.

I have known all along that perfect love has to be fatal. I have survived on four of the five continents. I get by because I am at least moderately charming and open-minded. From time to time, James Beamish calls me. "She's promised to file for divorce." Or "Let's go away for a weekend. Let's go to Bermuda. Have lunch with me this Wednesday." Why do I hear a second voice? She has laughed at me. She has mocked my passion.

I want to say yes. I want to beg him to take me away to Hilton Head in his new, retirement Winnebago. The golden light from the vista is too yellow. Yes, *please*, let's run away, keep this new and simple.

I can hear the golf balls being thwocked home by clumsy mummers far away where my land dips. My arms are numb, my breathing loud and ugly from pressing hard against the cedar railing. The pain in my chest will not go away. I should be tasting blood in my throat by now.

The World
According to Hsu

THEY had come to this island off the coast of Africa for simple reasons: he to see the Southern Cross and she to take stock of a life that had until recently seemed to her manageably capricious. Their travel agent, a refugee from Beirut, morbidly sensitive to political and epidemical tremors, had not warned them of the latest crisis in the capital. Coups and curfews visited with seasonal regularity, but like nearly everything else about the island, went unreported in the press. The most recent, involving melancholy students and ungenerous bureaucrats, had been especially ferocious; people had died and shops had been sacked but nothing had stained the island's reputation for languor and spices.

The Claytons did not blame Camille Lioon, the travel agent. No one could have told them about the revolution, this thing called, alternatively (in the island's morning daily), *les événements de soixante-dix-huit,* and *l'aventure des forces contre-revolutionnaires, impérialistes, et capitalistes.* Continents slide, no surface is permanent. Today's ballooning teenager is tomorrow's anorexic. The island should have been a paradise.

They had wanted an old-fashioned vacation on the shores of a vast new ocean. They had planned to pick shells, feed lemurs on the balcony of a hotel managed by a paunchy Indian, visit a colonial museum or two, where, under glass, the new guardians of the nation enshrined the whips and chains of their unnatural past. They had readied themselves for small misadventures— lost bags, cancelled hotel reservations—the kind that Graeme Clayton could tell with some charm on their return to Canada.

But Ratna Clayton, groping for the wisdom that should have descended on her in her thirty-third year, hoped for something more from this journey to the island below the equator. Surely simple tourist pleasures, for instance, watching the big pink sun fall nightly into calm pink waters, would lighten the shadows of the past six months? She imagined herself in her daring new bikini on a shoreline tangled with branches and cattle skulls. The landscape was always narcotically beautiful. But always, Graeme was just behind her, training his Nikon on that chaotic greenery to extract from it some definitive order.

In Montreal, each Ektachrome transparency of the island, she knew, would command a commentary, every slide a mini-lecture. Lecturing was Graeme's business. For his friends he would shape and reshape the tropical confusion. Ratna would serve her cashew-lamb pilaf and begin hesitant anecdotes about pickpockets and beggars. The friends would listen with civil, industrious faces until Graeme, having set up the projector, was free to entertain and instruct. The burned-out buses,

they would learn, were Hungarian; the plump young
paratroopers with flat African faces were coastal people, a reminder of the island's proximity to the Dark
Continent. The ducks in the rice paddies did not yet
answer to genus and species; Graeme would have to
look it up. And bitter, terrified, politicized Freddie Mc-
Laren, Graeme's colleague at McGill, would find an
opportune moment to pipe up, "I don't know why you
two went to Africa. If you wanted trouble you could've
found it right here in Canada." Freddie with his talk
of Belfast and Beirut, and what the future held for Montreal. "It's not going to matter one damn bit to them
that you speak French and hate Ontario as much as they
do," he'd say, and Graeme would answer, "But Freddie—I don't hate Ontario." Ratna Clayton would add,
quietly, "And I don't hate Quebec." And soon the
McLarens would lead the Claytons back from Africa
and its riots to the safe disasters of letter-bombs and
budget cuts.

Camille Lioon had prepared them for lesser dangers.
"No, m'sieur, you should not make the *escale* in Zan-
zibar, where I have heard there is much cholera." Camille had contacts in World Health, in banks, in
subministries around the world. Ratna pictured a small
army of sallow Lioons frenziedly sending telegrams to
all parts of the French-speaking world: *disaster immi-
nent. Don't come. Hide.* And to Ratna he'd whispered,
"No, madame, if I were Hindu I would cancel the *escale* in Jiddah. Those Saudis, they're so insensible."
Ratna smiled, suspecting that Camille had slipped on a
tangled cognate.

"Insensitive?" she'd asked.

"Yes, yes, insensitive."

"Unfeeling?" Ratna pursued.

"That's it! *Un peu brutale.*"

In Riyadh, chopped-off hands were lying on the street. The street was black with flies, feasting on hands, according to Camille. "I am no less an Arab than they, but if I land in Mecca—phfft—they slit my throat, no questions asked. Not even in anger. No, I would definitely not stop in Jiddah." The trouble with the Saudis, Graeme had thought, was not with their quaint notions of punishment. It was that they had lost some of their wayward mystery. In spite of their genial floggings and stoical dismemberments, petro-dollars had opened them up, made them accessible to Rotarians and the covers of *Time*. And so the Claytons had given up their earlier itinerary, not because Camille's caution was infectious, but because they yearned for once to be simple-minded travellers yielding to every expensive and off-beat prompting. This island of spices, this misplaced Tahiti, this gorgeous anachronism, would serve them beautifully, they'd thought.

Graeme had reserved his strength, which came to him in paroxysms much like panic, for this voyage of a lifetime to what everyone called *la grande île au bout du monde*. Islands and endings were Graeme's business too, and he demanded, in his leisure, a certain consonance with his discipline. He was thirty-five, the youngest full professor of psychology at McGill, an authority on a whole rainbow of dysfunctions, and he had a need for something which he in his old-fashioned way called romance. It was not the opposite of reality; it was more a sharpening of line and color, possible only in the labs or on a carefully researched, fully cooperative, tropical island. In the place of a heart he should have had a Nikon.

Besides, he hoped the vacation would be the right setting for persuading Ratna to move to Toronto, where he'd been offered—quite surprisingly in a year when English Montrealers would leap at just about anything—the chair in Personality Development. So far, she'd been obdurate. She claimed to be happy enough in Montreal, less perturbed by the impersonal revenges of Quebec politicians than personal attacks by Toronto racists. In Montreal she was merely ''English,'' a grim joke on generations of British segregationists. It was thought charming that her French was just slightly short of fluent. In Toronto, she was not Canadian, not even Indian. She was something called, after the imported idiom of London, a Paki. And for Pakis, Toronto was hell.

She had only a secondhand interest in the English language and a decided aversion to British institutions; English had been a mutually agreed upon second language in her home, in her first city, in her first country, in her career and it had remained so, even in her marriage. Frenchification was quaint, not threatening. She'd even voted for the separatists. She had claimed reluctance to chop off what tentative roots she had in Montreal. *La grande île* was to be a refuge from just such fruitless debates.

So, having picked their archipelago to get away to, the Claytons had flown in on schedule one wintry June morning (it was cool; sweater weather, though many of the islanders at the airport had been wearing overcoats, gloves and caps with tied-down earflaps) and immediately found themselves prisoners of an unreported revolution.

Their prison, a twenty-five dollar a day double room with a bath and bidet at the Hotel Papillon, was not uncomfortable. In a time of lesser crisis they might have complained, among themselves, of the lumps in the mattress or the pale stains on the towel. They might have wondered at the new gray wall-to-wall carpeting, the Simenon novels on the window ledge, the Cinzano ashtrays ("This is Africa? This is a People's Republic?"). But now, on their first day in the capital, still convalescing from thirty hours' flying and the teetering ride in the airport taxi, the Papillon appeared a triumph of French obstinacy in the face of antipodean distraction.

The entrance to the hotel, whose walls were ochre deepening to brown where the water pipes had rusted, was off a sidewalk choked with stalls. Around the entrance were pyramids of tomatoes, green peppers, dried fish, fried grasshoppers, safety pins and chipped buttons. The sidewalk directly in front of it was gouged and fissured, as though islanders walking by had wrenched up the paving stones and put them to more urgent, if unrecorded, use. The gouges were coated with the pulp of chewed rotting food spat out by the stall-keepers. An opaque glass door behind a sidewalk tangle of metal tables and chairs had announced in neat black lettering:

HOTEL PAPILLON
Prop: M J-P Papillon

Monsieur Jean-Paul Papillon, the Claytons learned from Justin, the taxi-driver, had died thirteen years before. The hotel had been declining with his health. Why hadn't they chosen the new Hilton? The Hilton was a touch of Paris.

"In the old days," Justin said, "this place was better than anything in Marseilles. The French called it the pearl of the Indian Ocean. The restaurant of the Papillon had two stars from Michelin." Then, turning to Ratna Clayton, he'd asked, "Do you want me to drive you to the Hilton?"

They had gotten off at the Papillon to spite the driver. To Justin, the Claytons had seemed American or German, part of the natural Hilton crowd. The Hilton had four dining rooms and a rooftop casino. From late October through to the beginning of autumn, in April, it maintained an outdoor pool. Graeme understood the type-casting and decided not to forgive him.

"Papillon," Graeme had ordered, having studied all the guide books on the flight from Paris. "L'avenue d'Albert Camus."

"M'sieur-dame, you don't understand," Justin had pleaded, placing a pink restraining palm on their luggage. "The Papillon is in the center of the marketplace."

"*Tant mieux,*" Ratna had said, nudging a suitcase out of his grip.

"But madame, *les manifesteurs* . . . there might be trouble again tonight."

"We'll manage," Graeme had said. Other people's revolutions could not shock or dismay. He wondered if tourists in Montreal, those few who still came, counted themselves equally bold.

"But m'sieur," Justin begged, now flushed from his coyness, "all the Indians, they stay at the Hilton. In times like these, it's the safest place."

"I am a Canadian," Ratna said arrogantly. "I'm a Canadian tourist and I want to stay at the Papillon in the marketplace, okay?"

The truth was, she knew, that even on this island she could not escape the consequences of being half—the dominant half—Indian. Her mother, a Czech nurse, had found love or perhaps only escape in a young Indian medical student on holiday in Europe in 1936, and she had sailed with him to Calcutta. She'd died there last year, a shrunken widow in a white sari, allegedly a happy woman. The European strain had appeared and disappeared, leaving no genetic souvenir (for her first two years, family legend had it, Ratna had been a pale, scrawny blonde, shunned by her father's family as a "white rat"). Ratna's Europeanness lay submerged like an ancient city waiting to be revealed by shallow-water archeology. Her show of unaccustomed fervor apparently satisfied Justin.

"Alors, madame, vous n'êtes pas indienne?" He had then swung the bag out of her hand and carried it to the hotel entrance.

"Are the nights cloudy in June?" Graeme had asked, paying him off. "I've come a long way to see the Southern Cross."

"That's when they'd learned the cruncher. Justin pointed to a hastily scrawled sign, pasted to the door. COUVRE-FEU 17h.

"All-night curfew, m'sieur. *Tout est fermé* . . . No stars, no nothing."

"God!" muttered Graeme Clayton.

"That explains those paratroopers tramping around the paddy-fields," Ratna remarked. She was a freelance journalist grateful for good copy. There had been para-

troopers everywhere, black faces from the coast, ubiq-
uitous sentinels among the copper-skinned, straw-hatted
natives of the capital. Descending on the adobe villages
like Van Gogh's crows, they had squatted in the clean
greenness of banana groves, kicked the muddy flanks
of water buffalo and sped down the airport road in their
frail Renaults. They had even stopped Justin's taxi a few
miles outside the city and ordered a half-hearted search
of the Claytons' baggage. She'd not realized, until seeing the curfew sign, that she and Graeme might have
been in danger, that the soldiers' comments in a different language, obviously directed to Justin about her,
could have led to untraceable tragedy in a paddy-field.

Justin seemed reluctant to leave them. "You want me
to come back for you this afternoon? I'll make you a
cheap excursion."

"How much?"

"Ten thousand francs. I'll give you the two-hour tour,
bring you back before the curfew."

Ratna had not yet calibrated the local currency. Ten
thousand was, roughly, thirty dollars. At the sound of
ten thousand she had snapped instinctively, "Too
much."

"Eight thousand."

"Come for us at three."

Still Justin hung around. He had become transformed
from taxi-driver to gracious host. She wondered if they
owed him their lives; that if they'd not been cheerful
and approving and engaging in that brief ride from the
airport to the informal roadblock, and if he had not said
something preventive to the troops, she and Graeme
would have been slaughtered, their travellers' checks
and local currency and Canadian dollars and gold chains

and Nikon apportioned as the usual supplemental wages.

The lobby was narrow, dark, no more than a corridor partitioned off the hotel's former dining room. Three islanders were still breakfasting on *café au lait*, croissants and a Gauloise: each at his table replicating France. Compared to them, Ratna thought, the Montrealers they had left behind at Charles de Gaulle Airport—those for whom Paris and not the end of the world had been the destination—were nothing but wonderstruck Americans, accidental French-speakers with Quebec fleurs-de-lis sewn on their bulging hip pockets. Far less Gallic than these Peruvian-looking Africans waiting out another bizarre crisis at the Papillon.

The proprietress sat at the end of the dark corridor, behind an uneven counter and under a cardboard arrow that said: Caisse. She was obese, with densely powdered, flour-white skin.

Justin preceded the Canadians. He asked first after Madame Papillon's daughter, who had apparently been sent back to France for *traitements*. Treatments for what? Graeme was about to ask, then suppressed it. Madame Papillon asked Justin about *les événements*: had there been much looting? He reassured her. Nothing new. Only two blocks burned. The epicenter of the looting was only a block away; Madame Papillon was evidently reclusive. The shops of the Indians in la Place de l'Indépendance and along the Faubourg. *Les indiens*, they had fled as usual to the Hilton, to lock up their gold and money in the hotel's safe. *"Ah, toujours les indiens,"* wheezed Madame, *"les juifs de l'Afrique."* Students were gathering again in front of the Secretariat building. Possibly, another outbreak might occur that night. (Later, during the sightseeing trip, Justin explained that Madame Papillon, a model of Vichy rectitude, had not stepped from the hotel since her husband's death thirteen years before. "I bring her news like infusions," he said.)

After the bellboy had left, cautioning them that the tap water was not potable and that mineral water could be secured through him more cheaply than through room service, they forced open the window shutters for their first private view of the city.

"Don't worry about the smoke," Graeme said. "The fires are out."

"I'm not worrying about this island," Ratna said from the closet where she was checking the wallpaper seams for roaches. "I'm worrying about Toronto." A week before their flight, a Bengali woman was beaten and nearly blinded on the street. And the week before that an eight-year-old Punjabi boy was struck by a car announcing on its bumper: KEEP CANADA GREEN. PAINT A PAKI.

He knew from the deadness of her voice what was to come. "It won't happen to you," he said quickly. He resented this habit she had of injecting bitterness into every new scene. He had paid five thousand dollars in airfare so they could hold hands on a beach under the Southern Cross, but already she was accusing him of selfishness and bigotry.

"That's not the point."

"Look—violence is everywhere. Toronto's the safest city on the continent."

"Sure," she said, "for you." She hung a cotton dress in the closet. She had married him for a trivial reason—his blue eyes—then discovered in him tenderness, affection, decency. Once not long ago she had believed in the capacity of these virtues to restore symmetry to lives mangled by larger, blunter antipathies. "An Indian professor's wife was jumped at a red light, right in her car. They threw her groceries on the street. They said Pakis shouldn't drive big cars."

"If you don't want to go to Toronto, we won't go."

"But you want to go. It's the best place for you. You said Montreal's finished."

"Can we just relax and enjoy the vacation?"

Ratna nodded. He deserved a truce.

Justin returned for them at 3:05. He had borrowed his brother's Peugeot. His brother sold polished stones; he could give them a good price. He drove them to a lookout point near an old French fort. The city lay spilled over the greenish-red hills like bushels of stone eggs, clinging to ledges and piling up in colorful heaps in the valleys. In the afternoon light, the oranges and yellows of the buildings were brilliant. They counted thirty-seven churches, Lutheran predominating. "Swedish missionaries in the 19th century," Justin explained. "Very successful, before the massacre." Graeme asked if all the islanders were Christian, and Justin said they were; religion was called *la troisième force*. They were reluctant to inquire about the first two. *"Mais les peuples de côte nord, ils sont un peu musulman au même temps."*

The heat of the June sun was gentle. The people wore their winter clothes capriciously, as though experimenting with other nations' castoffs. It was hard to think of them as revolutionaries, but in that morning's paper, the riots of the night before had been termed counterrevolutionary, the work of enemies of the revolution, fueled by agents of international capitalism. The only foreign country with influence besides France, according to Justin, was North Korea.

He showed them the legitimate sights: the President's house, the squares where various presidents had been assassinated or executed, a housing project, an artificial lake and the Hilton Hotel which was the tallest building in the city.

The zoo was closed to the public because of the disturbances. The museum too was closed indefinitely. The mission school, run by Quebec fathers, was closed. At the Monday market they walked around two burned trucks and bought mangoes.

Finally, Justin said, "If you like, we can drive past the Indian shops."

They drove behind a truckload of jeering paratroopers who pointed their rifles and fired mock salvos into their taxi. Justin appeared worried and Graeme cringed, but Ratna felt safer than she had in the subway stations of Toronto. They swung onto a wide boulevard, la Place de l'Indépendance, lined with gutted shops. In one ruined shop, a mannequin in lavender silk stuck an intact head out of a jagged hole in the display case. The signboard was splashed with tomatoes:

LUI ET ELLIE
Importeurs
Props. K. Mourardji Desai et Fils

A paratrooper, daubed in garish greens and browns, waved them on.

"Drive slowly," Graeme whispered. He hid his Nikon half in his shirt and snapped the paratrooper beside the mannequin.

Justin had promised them a two-hour trip but he had shown them the city in forty-five minutes. Too many things were closed, too many sections of town under guard. So they asked him to drive out into the country.

For miles the road was nothing more than an untidy gash, an aid-project miscalculation, on the side of an endless red hill. They feared the road might strand them among wet rice fields and blood-red adobes. Then, without warning, the flaccid gash acquired a scab of gray; it became an oddly formal *grande allée* wider than a runway, lined with jacaranda and light standards. The boulevard terminated at the iron gate of a wooden house with painted columns.

"Et voilà," Justin announced. *"Le palais de roi."*

"Where's the King?" Ratna asked.

"The French threw him out in 1767. He was seven feet tall and used to kill missionaries by biting their heads off—phfft."

"Where's that music coming from?" Graeme asked. Faint, almost familiar, it seemed to be coming from the royal grounds.

"Oh, that? It is a recital by the King's band."

"But you have no king."

"We still have his band. Only the best musicians are allowed to play."

"It is open to the public?"

"No, no," said Justin, throwing up his hands. "The public is not allowed. No photography is allowed."

"Then who the hell are they playing for? Are they practicing for a special occasion?"

"Yes, they are rehearsing," said Justin.

"For a holiday?"

"No, no, the revolution outlawed all the old holidays. Now they give recitals here everyday."

"For themselves?" asked Ratna.

"Yes, yes, only for themselves. They rehearse for when the holidays come back and they give recitals everyday for themselves."

The Claytons walked up the shallow steps that led to the iron gate. Heavy chains and an ornamental lock were looped around its rusty trelliswork. It was hard to think of that entrance or of that wooden house as royal. There were no guards, not even the gaudy paratroopers in open-topped boots. The Claytons searched the wooden structure—the wood turned out to be just a facade for another large adobe box—for clues to its forgotten history, but all the plaques had been taken down. The walls showed no flags, no heraldic signs, not even the mysterious wounds of battle. Over to one side, under the shade of jacaranda trees, sat the King's band. Their uniforms were splendidly gallant, red satin with gold braid. It was a brass band; the bandmaster wore a yachting cap and a bright red tunic. His white beard was neatly trimmed. The band knew the piece well, whatever it was; this was a recital, not a practice. The notes meandered in the wintry twilight, refusing to coalesce into anything familiar. The music revealed no hurt, no quiet suffering—it was intended for pomp and public celebration, it was music of the plazas and reviewing stands. The moment held no pathos, only dust and gallantry. When the visitors had to leave because it was too perilously close to the curfew deadline, the man playing the tuba tipped his instrument in Ratna's direction.

* * *

At 5:30, Madame Papillon taped down the windows of the dining hall so that even if stones were thrown later that night, the glass would not shatter. At 6:30, she locked the glass-fronted entrance to the hotel. At seven, the Claytons came down for dinner.

Graeme brought his copy of *Scientific American* that he had begun to read on the plane. This was his light reading; he had brought no psych or medical journals with him.

"Did you know that it's always irritated me, I mean your reading at the table?"

"I'm not reading," he said, meaning *you're free to interrupt me, I'm not advancing my career; I'm being open and conversational, this is just the sports page to me.* "Did you know, according to . . ."

She couldn't catch the name, but it sounded like a dry sneeze. Hsü? Could it be Hsü?

". . . that six million years ago the Mediterranean basin was a desert? And it took the Atlantic a million years to break through and fill it again? Gibraltar for a million years was the most spectacular waterfall the world will ever see. The old sea was called Tethys and it connected the Atlantic with the Indian Ocean."

At the table to her right a German communications expert was teaching an English folksong to three Ismaili-Indian children.

"Row, row, row your boat," the children shouted, before collapsing in giggles.

"In the last Ice Age the Black Sea was a freshwater lake. They have fossil crustaceans to prove it."

The children's father, a small handsome man, scraped his chair back and said, "Watch me. Here is Bob Hope playing golf.'' The children giggled again. How, Ratna wondered, how in the world had they seen or heard of Bob Hope? Or golf? Or had they, or did it matter? It struck her as unspeakably heroic, gallant.

Graeme asked her if she was crying.

An American at the next table looked up at her from the paperback he was pretending to read and winked at her. He was tanned like a marine biologist.

Graeme slid the magazine across to her. She read the title: ''When the Black Sea Was Drained,'' by Kenneth J. Hsü.

''He writes very well,'' said Graeme. This, she realized, was a concession to her; he was appreciating something remotely journalistic, though still respectably scientific.

An African chef, in a flowered shirt, carried a casserole to their table. Ratna had ordered ''the National Dish.'' She found it a concoction of astonishing crudity.

A waiter turned on the television set for the World Cup scores, relayed from Dar es Salaam, *en provenance de* Buenos Aires, on another cold night under the Southern Cross. The Claytons had not expected color television on such an island. The German (East or West, Ratna wondered), overhearing the Canadians, informed them that it was cheaper to install the latest color system than an obsolete black-and-white one. It had to do with the island's profound underdevelopment. They could not even manufacture their own spare parts, and the industrialized countries no longer turned out components for black-and-white. That's why he was on the island, he said; to install a complete microwave transmitting system. Given her mood, it struck Ratna as one of the most brutal stories she had ever heard.

"What about India?" she asked.

"Oh, India is technologically sophisticated," he said. And she was faintly, absurdly, assured. India would keep its sophisticated black-and-white system for the foreseeable future and leave color to the basket-cases.

A woman news announcer said in carefully articulated French that there had been a coup on a nearby archipelago. Counterrevolutionary forces led by neo-colonialist intriguers had killed the popular, progressive prime minister and placed the islands under martial law. Progressive people everywhere expressed their concern, and from Pyong-yang, Kim Il Sung spoke for the whole world in denouncing this act of capitalist desperation. Demonstrations in support of the true revolutionaries would be held tomorrow in the capital, at the municipal football stadium. No mention was made of the riots on the island, which led Graeme to speculate that things were getting worse.

"According to Hsü," he said, "the last time the world was one must have been about six million years ago. Now Africa and Asia are colliding. India got smashed into Asia—that's why the Himalayas got wrinkled up. This island is just part of the debris."

Ratna played with forkfuls of the national dish. Why did the Black Sea have to drain? Why did continents have to collide? Why did they have to move to Toronto?

On that small island, in that besieged dining hall, she felt that with effort she might become an expert on the plate tectonics of emotion. As long as she could sit and listen to the other guests converse in a mutually agreed-upon second language, she would be all right. Like her, they were non-islanders, refugees.

She heard Graeme ask Madame Papillon, "Is it safe to go outside for a moment? I've spent a fortune to see the Southern Cross."

At nine, while they were lingering over a local red wine, a waiter burst in with news. Snipers had shot the Bulgarian ambassador's wife. She had been watching the riot from her balcony and phfft—a sniper had got her in the chest. Now the paratroopers would probably go on a rampage.

"It's always the same thing," Madame Papillon sighed. "The students want to overthrow the government. You can't carry on an honest business on this island." She left, to sit again at her desk.

Graeme poured more wine, draining the bottle. "An acceptable red wine—surprising, eh, from such a place?"

"It used to be French," Ratna said. At least the French left palpable legacies, despite the profound underdevelopment.

"By the way," Graeme said, "I wrote to Toronto before we left. I've accepted the Chair. And don't worry, if anything happens to you there I promise we'll leave. Immediately, okay?"

"What can I say?"

"Will you come see the stars with me?"

"Not tonight."

He signaled for the waiter and ordered another half-bottle of red wine. He poured her a glass, then called the waiter back. She heard the waiter mention *La Voie lactée* and *les sacs de charbon,* and Graeme's eyes lit up. "The Coalsack! I didn't think I'd ever see it." And just below the coal sacks in that luminous tropical Milky Way, low on the horizon, the waiter told him he'd see the Southern Cross.

They went out, through the kitchen and the service entrance.

He'd be all right, she thought. Wherever he went.

The American leaned toward her from his table. "What's this," he asked, "this *champignons farcis*?" He looked drunk, but courteous. She had to look where he was pointing.

"Mushrooms," she said, smiling. From that odd opening on that odd island a conversation could go anywhere. Not all North Americans were forced to fear the passionate consequences of their unilingualism.

For the first time she saw that the label on the bottle read: Côte de Cassandre. A superior red table wine that no one had ever heard of; perhaps the lone competent industry on the island. Better, she thought, than the Quebec cider she and Graeme made such a patriotic point of always serving.

She poured herself another glass, feeling for the moment at home in that collection of Indians and Europeans babbling in English and remembered dialects. No matter where she lived, she would never feel so at home again.

A Father

ONE Wednesday morning in mid-May Mr. Bhowmick woke up as he usually did at 5:43 a.m., checked his Rolex against the alarm clock's digital readout, punched down the alarm (set for 5:45), then nudged his wife awake. She worked as a claims investigator for an insurance company that had an office in a nearby shopping mall. She didn't really have to leave the house until 8:30, but she liked to get up early and cook him a big breakfast. Mr. Bhowmick had to drive a long way to work. He was a naturally dutiful, cautious man, and he set the alarm clock early enough to accommodate a margin for accidents.

While his wife, in a pink nylon negligee she had paid for with her own MasterCard card, made him a new version of French toast from a clipping ("Eggs-cellent Recipes!") Scotchtaped to the inside of a kitchen cupboard, Mr. Bhowmick brushed his teeth. He brushed, he gurgled with the loud, hawking noises that he and his brother had been taught as children to make in order to flush clean not merely teeth but also tongue and palate.

After that he showered, then, back in the bedroom again, he recited prayers in Sanskrit to Kali, the patron goddess of his family, the goddess of wrath and vengeance. In the pokey flat of his childhood in Ranchi, Bihar, his mother had given over a whole bedroom to her collection of gods and goddesses. Mr. Bhowmick couldn't be that extravagant in Detroit. His daughter, twenty-six and an electrical engineer, slept in the other of the two bedrooms in his apartment. But he had done his best. He had taken Woodworking I and II at a nearby recreation center and built a grotto for the goddess. Kali-Mata was eight inches tall, made of metal and painted a glistening black so that the metal glowed like the oiled, black skin of a peasant woman. And though Kali-Mata was totally nude except for a tiny gilt crown and a garland strung together from sinners' chopped off heads, she looked warm, cozy, *pleased*, in her make-shift wooden shrine in Detroit. Mr. Bhowmick had gathered quite a crowd of admiring, fellow woodworkers in those final weeks of decoration.

"Hurry it up with the prayers," his wife shouted from the kitchen. She was an agnostic, a believer in ambition, not grace. She frequently complained that his prayers had gotten so long that soon he wouldn't have time to go to work, play duplicate bridge with the Ghosals, or play the tabla in the Bengali Association's one Sunday per month musical soirees. Lately she'd begun to drain him in a wholly new way. He wasn't praying, she nagged; he was shutting her out of his life. There'd be no place in the house until she hid Kali-Mata in a suitcase.

She nagged, and he threatened to beat her with his

shoe as his father had threatened his mother: it was the thrust and volley of marriage. There was no question of actually taking off a shoe and applying it to his wife's body. She was bigger than he was. And, secretly, he admired her for having the nerve, the agnosticism, which as a college boy in backward Bihar he too had claimed.

"I have time," he shot at her. He was still wrapped in a damp terry towel.

"You have time for everything but domestic life."

It was the fault of the shopping mall that his wife had started to buy pop psychology paperbacks. These paperbacks preached that for couples who could sit down and talk about their "relationship," life would be sweet again. His engineer daughter was on his wife's side. She accused him of holding things in.

"Face it, Dad," she said. "You have an affect deficit."

But surely everyone had feelings they didn't want to talk about or talk over. He definitely did not want to blurt out anything about the sick-in-the-guts sensations that came over him most mornings and that he couldn't bubble down with Alka-Seltzer or smother with Gas-X. The women in his family were smarter than him. They were cheerful, outgoing, more American somehow.

How could he tell these bright, mocking women that in the 5:43 a.m. darkness, he sensed invisible presences: gods and snakes frolicked in the master bedroom, little white sparks of cosmic static crackled up the legs of his pajamas. Something was out there in the dark, something that could invent accidents and coincidences to remind mortals that even in Detroit they were no more than mortal. His wife would label this paranoia and dismiss it. Paranoia, premonition: whatever it was, it had begun to undermine his composure.

Take this morning, Mr. Bhowmick had woken up from a pleasant dream about a man taking a Club Med vacation, and the postdream satisfaction had lasted through the shower, but when he'd come back to the shrine in the bedroom, he'd noticed all at once how scarlet and saucy was the tongue that Kali-Mata stuck out at the world. Surely he had not lavished such alarming detail, such admonitory colors on that flap of flesh.

Watch out, ambulatory sinners. Be careful out there, the goddess warned him, and not with the affection of Sergeant Esterhaus, either.

"French toast must be eaten hot-hot," his wife nagged. "Otherwise they'll taste like rubber."

Mr. Bhowmick laid the trousers of a two-trouser suit he had bought on sale that winter against his favorite tweed jacket. The navy stripes in the trousers and the small, navy tweed flecks in the jacket looked quite good together. So what if the Chief Engineer had already started wearing summer cottons?

"I am coming, I am coming," he shouted back. "You want me to eat hot-hot, you start the frying only when I am sitting down. You didn't learn anything from Mother in Ranchi?"

"Mother cooked French toast from fancy recipes? I mean French Sandwich Toast with complicated filling?"

He came into the room to give her his testiest look. "You don't know the meaning of complicated cookery.

And mother had to get the coal fire of the *chula* going first.''

His daughter was already at the table. ''Why don't you break down and buy her a microwave oven? That's what I mean about sitting down and talking things out.'' She had finished her orange juice. She took a plastic measure of Slim-Fast out of its can and poured the powder into a glass of skim milk. ''It's ridiculous.''

Babli was not the child he would have chosen as his only heir. She was brighter certainly than the sons and daughters of the other Bengalis he knew in Detroit, and she had been the only female student in most of her classes at Georgia Tech, but as she sat there in her beige linen business suit, her thick chin dropping into a polka-dotted cravat, he regretted again that she was not the child of his dreams. Babli would be able to help him out moneywise if something happened to him, something so bad that even his pension plans and his insurance policies and his money market schemes wouldn't be enough. But Babli could never comfort him. She wasn't womanly or tender the way that unmarried girls had been in the wistful days of his adolescence. She could sing Hindi film songs, mimicking exactly the high, artificial voice of Lata Mungeshkar, and she had taken two years of dance lessons at Sona Devi's Dance Academy in Southfield, but these accomplishments didn't add up to real femininity. Not the kind that had given him palpitations in Ranchi.

Mr. Bhowmick did his best with his wife's French toast. In spite of its filling of marshmallows, apricot jam and maple syrup, it tasted rubbery. He drank two cups of Darjeeling tea, said, ''Well, I'm off,'' and took off.

All might have gone well if Mr. Bhowmick hadn't fussed longer than usual about putting his briefcase and his trenchcoat in the backseat. He got in behind the wheel of his Oldsmobile, fixed his seatbelt and was just about to turn the key in the ignition when his neighbor, Al Stazniak, who was starting up his Buick Skylark, sneezed. A sneeze at the start of a journey brings bad luck. Al Stazniak's sneeze was fierce, made up of five short bursts, too loud to be ignored.

Be careful out there! Mr. Bhowmick could see the goddess's scarlet little tongue tip wagging at him.

He was a modern man, an intelligent man. Otherwise he couldn't have had the options in life that he did have. He couldn't have given up a good job with perks in Bombay and found a better job with General Motors in Detroit. But Mr. Bhowmick was also a prudent enough man to know that some abiding truth lies bunkered within each wanton Hindu superstition. A sneeze was more than a sneeze. The heedless are carried off in ambulances. He had choices to make. He could ignore the sneeze, and so challenge the world unseen by men. Perhaps Al Stazniak had hayfever. For a sneeze to be a potent omen, surely it had to be unprovoked and terrifying, a thunderclap cleaving the summer skies. Or he could admit the smallness of mortals, undo the fate of the universe by starting over, and go back inside the apartment, sit for a second on the sofa, then re-start his trip.

Al Stazniak rolled down his window. "Everything okay?"

Mr. Bhowmick nodded shyly. They weren't really friends in the way neighbors can sometimes be. They talked as they parked or pulled out of their adjacent

parking stalls. For all Mr. Bhowmick knew, Al Stazniak had no legs. He had never seen the man out of his
Skylark.

He let the Buick back out first. Everything was okay,
yes, please. All the same he undid his seatbelt. Com-
promise, adaptability, call it what you will. A dozen
times a day he made these small trade-offs between new-
world reasonableness and old-world beliefs.

While he was sitting in his parked car, his wife's ride
came by. For fifty dollars a month, she was picked up
and dropped off by a hard up, newly divorced woman
who worked at a florist's shop in the same mall. His
wife came out the front door in brown K-Mart pants
and a burgundy windbreaker. She waved to him, then
slipped into the passenger seat of the florist's rusty Japanese car.

He was a metallurgist. He knew about rust and ways of
preventing it, secret ways, thus far unknown to the Japanese.

Babli's fiery red Mitsubishi was still in the lot. She
wouldn't leave for work for another eight minutes. He
didn't want her to know he'd been undone by a sneeze.
Babli wasn't tolerant of superstitions. She played New
Wave music in her tapedeck. If asked about Hinduism,
all she'd ever said to her American friends was that "it's
neat." Mr. Bhowmick had heard her on the phone years
before. The cosmos balanced on the head of a snake
was like a beachball balanced on the snout of a circus
seal. "This Hindu myth stuff," he'd heard her say, "is
like a series of super graphics."

He'd forgiven her. He could probably forgive her anything. It was her way of surviving high school in a city
that was both native to her, and alien.

There was no question of going back where he'd come
from. He hated Ranchi. Ranchi was no place for dream-
ers. All through his teenage years, Mr. Bhowmick had
dreamed of success abroad. What form that success
would take he had left vague. Success had meant to him
escape from the constant plotting and bitterness that
wore out India's middle class.

Babli should have come out of the apartment and
driven off to work by now. Mr. Bhowmick decided to
take a risk, to dash inside and pretend he'd left his briefcase on the coffee table.

When he entered the living room, he noticed Babli's
spring coat and large vinyl pocketbook on the sofa. She
was probably sorting through the junk jewelry on her
dresser to give her business suit a lift. She read hints
about dressing in women's magazines and applied them
to her person with seriousness. If his luck held, he could
sit on the sofa, say a quick prayer and get back to the
car without her catching on.

It surprised him that she didn't shout out from her bedroom, "Who's there?" What if he had been a rapist?

Then he heard Babli in the bathroom. He heard un-
ladylike squawking noises. She was throwing up. A
squawk, a spitting, then the horrible gurgle of a waterfall.

A revelation came to Mr. Bhowmick. A woman vom-
iting in the privacy of the bathroom could mean many
things. She was coming down with the flu. She was
nervous about a meeting. But Mr. Bhowmick knew at
once that his daughter, his untender, unloving daughter
whom he couldn't love and hadn't tried to love, was
not, in the larger world of Detroit, unloved. Sinners are
everywhere, even in the bosom of an upright, unambi-

tious family like the Bhowmicks. It was the goddess sticking out her tongue at him.

The father sat heavily on the sofa, shrinking from contact with her coat and pocketbook. His brisk, bright engineer daughter was pregnant. Someone had taken time to make love to her. Someone had thought her tender, feminine. Someone even now was perhaps mooning over her. The idea excited him. It was so grotesque and wondrous. At twenty-six Babli had found the man of her dreams; whereas at twenty-six Mr. Bhowmick had given up on truth, beauty and poetry and exchanged them for two years at Carnegie Tech.

Mr. Bhowmick's tweed-jacketed body sagged against the sofa cushions. Babli would abort, of course. He knew his Babli. It was the only possible option if she didn't want to bring shame to the Bhowmick family. All the same, he could see a chubby baby boy on the rug, crawling to his granddaddy. Shame like that was easier to hide in Ranchi. There was always a barren womb sanctified by marriage that could claim sudden fructifying by the goddess Parvati. Babli would do what she wanted. She was headstrong and independent and he was afraid of her.

Babli staggered out of the bathroom. Damp stains ruined her linen suit. It was the first time he had seen his daughter look ridiculous, quite unprofessional. She didn't come into the living room to investigate the noises he'd made. He glimpsed her shoeless stockinged feet flip-flop on collapsed arches down the hall to her bedroom.

"Are you all right?" Mr. Bhowmick asked, standing in the hall. "Do you need Sinutab?"

She wheeled around. "What're you doing here?"

He was the one who should be angry. "I'm feeling poorly too," he said. "I'm taking the day off."

"I feel fine," Babli said.

Within fifteen minutes Babli had changed her clothes and left. Mr. Bhowmick had the apartment to himself all day. All day for praising or cursing the life that had brought him along with its other surprises an illegitimate grandchild.

It was his wife that he blamed. Coming to America to live had been his wife's idea. After the wedding, the young Bhowmicks had spent two years in Pittsburgh on his student visa, then gone back home to Ranchi for nine years. Nine crushing years. Then the job in Bombay had come through. All during those nine years his wife had screamed and wept. She was a woman of wild, progressive ideas—she'd called them her "American" ideas—and she'd been martyred by her neighbors for them. American *memsahib. Markin mem, Markin mem.* In bazaars the beggar boys had trailed her and hooted. She'd done provocative things. She'd hired a *chamar* woman who by caste rules was forbidden to cook for higher caste families, especially for widowed mothers of decent men. This had caused a blowup in the neighborhood. She'd made other, lesser errors. While other wives shopped and cooked every day, his wife had cooked the whole week's menu on weekends.

"What's the point of having a refrigerator, then?" She'd been scornful of the Ranchi women.

His mother, an old-fashioned widow, had accused her of trying to kill her by poisoning. "You are in such a hurry? You want to get rid of me quick-quick so you can go back to the States?"

Family life had been turbulent.

He had kept aloof, inwardly siding with his mother. He did not love his wife now, and he had not loved her then. In any case, he had not defended her. He felt some affection, and he felt guilty for having shunned her during those unhappy years. But he had thought of it then as revenge. He had wanted to marry a beautiful woman. Not being a young man of means, only a young man with prospects, he had had no right to yearn for pure beauty. He cursed his fate and after a while, settled for a barrister's daughter, a plain girl with a wide, flat plank of a body and myopic eyes. The barrister had sweetened the deal by throwing in an all-expenses-paid two years' study at Carnegie Tech to which Mr. Bhowmick had been admitted. Those two years had changed his wife from pliant girl to ambitious woman. She wanted America, nothing less.

It was his wife who had forced him to apply for permanent resident status in the U.S. even though he had a good job in Ranchi as a government engineer. The putting together of documents for the immigrant visa had been a long and humbling process. He had had to explain to a chilly clerk in the Embassy that, like most Indians of his generation, he had no birth certificate. He had to swear out affidavits, suffer through police checks, bribe orderlies whose job it was to move his dossier from desk to desk. The decision, the clerk had advised him, would take months, maybe years. He hadn't dared hope that merit might be rewarded. Merit could collapse under bad luck. It was for grace that he prayed.

While the immigration papers were being processed, he had found the job in Bombay. So he'd moved his mother in with his younger brother's family, and left his hometown for good. Life in Bombay had been light-hearted, almost fulfilling. His wife had thrown herself into charity work with the same energy that had offended the Ranchi women. He was happy to be in a big city at last. Bombay was the Rio de Janeiro of the East; he'd read that in a travel brochure. He drove out to Nariman Point at least once a week to admire the necklace of municipal lights, toss coconut shells into the dark ocean, drink beer at the Oberoi-Sheraton where overseas Indian girls in designer jeans beckoned him in sly ways. His nights were full. He played duplicate bridge, went to the movies, took his wife to Bingo nights at his club. In Detroit he was a lonelier man.

Then the green card had come through. For him, for his wife, and for the daughter who had been born to them in Bombay. He sold what he could sell, and put in his brother's informal trust what he couldn't to save on taxes. Then he had left for America, and one more start.

All through the week, Mr. Bhowmick watched his daughter. He kept furtive notes on how many times she rushed to the bathroom and made hawking, wrenching noises, how many times she stayed late at the office, calling her mother to say she'd be taking in a movie and pizza afterwards with friends.

He had to tell her that he knew. And he probably didn't have much time. She shouldn't be on Slim-Fast in her condition. He had to talk things over with her. But what would he say to her? What position could he take? He had to choose between public shame for the family, and murder.

For three more weeks he watched her and kept his

silence. Babli wore shifts to the office instead of business suits, and he liked her better in those garments. Perhaps she was dressing for her young man, not from necessity. Her skin was pale and blotchy by turn. At breakfast her fingers looked stiff, and she had trouble with silverware.

Two Saturdays running, he lost badly at duplicate bridge. His wife scolded him. He had made silly mistakes. When was Babli meeting this man? Where? He must be American; Mr. Bhowmick prayed only that he was white. He pictured his grandson crawling to him, and the grandson was always fat and brown and buttery-skinned, like the infant Krishna. An American son-in-law was a terrifying notion. Why was she not mentioning men, at least, preparing the way for the major announcement? He listened sharply for men's names, rehearsed little lines like, "Hello, Bob, I'm Babli's old man," with a cracked little laugh. Bob, Jack, Jimmy, Tom. But no names surfaced. When she went out for pizza and a movie it was with the familiar set of Indian girls and their strange, unpopular, American friends, all without men. Mr. Bhowmick tried to be reasonable. Maybe she had already gotten married and was keeping it secret. "Well, Bob, you and Babli sure had Mrs. Bhowmick and me going there, heh-heh," he mumbled one night with the Sahas and Ghosals, over cards. "Pardon?" asked Pronob Saha. Mr. Bhowmick dropped two tricks, and his wife glared. "Such stupid blunders," she fumed on the drive back. A new truth was dawning; there would be no marriage for Babli. Her young man probably was not so young and not so available. He must be already married. She must have yielded to passion or been raped in the office. His wife seemed to have noticed nothing. Was he a murderer, or a conspirator? He kept his secret from his wife; his daughter kept her decision to herself.

Nights, Mr. Bhowmick pretended to sleep, but as soon as his wife began her snoring—not real snores so much as loud, gaspy gulpings for breath—he turned on his side and prayed to Kali-Mata.

In July, when Babli's belly had begun to push up against the waistless dresses she'd bought herself, Mr. Bhowmick came out of the shower one weekday morning and found the two women screaming at each other. His wife had a rolling pin in one hand. His daughter held up a *National Geographic* as a shield for her head. The crazy look that had been in his wife's eyes when she'd shooed away beggar kids was in her eyes again.

"Stop it!" His own boldness overwhelmed him. "Shut up! Babli's pregnant, so what? It's your fault, you made us come to the States."

Girls like Babli were caught between rules, that's the point he wished to make. They were too smart, too impulsive for a backward place like Ranchi, but not tough nor smart enough for sex-crazy places like Detroit.

"My fault?" his wife cried. "I told her to do hanky-panky with boys? I told her to shame us like this?"

She got in one blow with the rolling pin. The second glanced off Babli's shoulder and fell on his arm which he had stuck out for his grandson's sake.

"I'm calling the police," Babli shouted. She was out of the rolling pin's range. "This is brutality. You can't do this to me."

"Shut up! Shut your mouth, foolish woman." He

wrenched the weapon from his wife's fist. He made a show of taking off his shoe to beat his wife on the face.

"What do you know? You don't know anything." She let herself down slowly on a dining chair. Her hair, curled overnight, stood in wild whorls around her head. "Nothing."

"And you do!" He laughed. He remembered her tormentors, and laughed again. He had begun to enjoy himself. Now *he* was the one with the crazy, progressive ideas.

"Your daughter is pregnant, yes," she said, "any fool knows that. But ask her the name of the father. Go, ask."

He stared at his daughter who gazed straight ahead, eyes burning with hate, jaw clenched with fury.

"Babli?"

"Who needs a man?" she hissed. "The father of my baby is a bottle and a syringe. Men louse up your lives. I just want a baby. Oh, don't worry—he's a certified fit donor. No diseases, college graduate, above average, and he made the easiest twenty-five dollars of his life—"

"Like animals," his wife said. For the first time he heard horror in her voice. His daughter grinned at him. He saw her tongue, thick and red, squirming behind her row of perfect teeth.

"Yes, yes, yes," she screamed, "like livestock. Just like animals. You should be happy—that's what marriage is all about, isn't it? Matching bloodlines, matching horoscopes, matching castes, matching, matching, matching . . ." and it was difficult to know if she was laughing or singing, or mocking and like a madwoman.

Mr. Bhowmick lifted the rolling pin high above his

head and brought it down hard on the dome of Babli's stomach. In the end, it was his wife who called the police.

Isolated Incidents

SEVEN years before, on a cool afternoon in May, the two girls had come out of the musty warmth of Miss Edgar's and Miss Cramp's and straggled down a leafy Westmount street to their separate futures. Poppy had done better than Ann. She called herself Peppi now—Peppi Paluka and the Pistolettes—and wore leather muscle-shirts and fearless disco pants. Through the listless years at McGill, Ann had kept a scrapbook: of Poppy stroking a cat in the lobby of the Beverly Hilton, of Poppy kissing Mike Douglas, of Poppy driving something sleek and low on the mad freeways of Los Angeles. "You can take the girl out of Canada," said Peppi Paluka in a promotional for her first CBC Special, "but you can't take Canada out of the girl, no way!"

Poppy had been wearing her "Fuddle Duddle" T-shirt. "Fuddle Duddle" had been her first hit single. Around that time Ann had inherited a little money from her Aunt Nellie, moved to Toronto (ahead of the rush) and had her heart broken by a feckless condo promoter.

Now Ann and Poppy were in the same city again. Ann had seen a picture of the Pistolettes in the *Star*. "I miss Canada," Peppi had said, "I really do. I miss everything about Canada, you know. I miss the good manners, the plodding, the uncrowdedness." You'll love her, too, the *Star* predicted, you'll love her gutsy, grungy performance. Poppy had called Ann—"Let's have a quick salad at least"—and Ann had agreed to meet her for lunch at her hotel.

All morning Ann sat at her corner desk in a large office, trying to hide her nervousness. Definitely, she told herself, she would not ask silly questions. It would just be two old friends, two professional women, two Westmount girls who'd been brought up to handle any social situation. But, my God, Poppy was a celebrity now. She had limos and a house in some dangerous Los Angeles canyon. She had a swimming pool laid out to resemble something ornate or disgusting, she couldn't remember which. She'd spent eight thousand dollars at the Eaton Centre the night before. "Mostly presents. I don't need anything for myself."

Ann's supervisor, Gladys Wakamatsu, had to ask twice for the file on recent incidents in the subway, and Bella Herzog went on for longer than usual about her husband's chest pains before Ann could pull together her practiced look of demure commiseration. She'd been gathering data on the Supariwala case. Doctor (Miss) Supariwala was a stern, stocky woman of forty-three, with doctorates from Western Ontario and Bombay, who claimed to have been passed over at job interviews in favor of lesser candidates. She was a Canadian citizen, she'd published numerous articles, she'd won a few research grants. No one could fault her promptness, her discipline, her preparedness. Against these accomplishments were arrayed certain half-articulated, coded objections. Students would not relate easily to her, some might complain of her accent, her methodological stiffness, her lack of humor. *My social poise and my good humour might be enhanced,* Dr. Supariwala had written, *if I had a position commensurate with my training.* "She belongs to the world of research, not of the classroom," wrote one chairman, adding shyly, "like many of her countrywomen." "She should apply to StatsCan," said another. "Sing-song accent." "The university year is a six-month voyage in a first-class stateroom," wrote another, choosing the higher road. "Surely we have a right to choose our companions carefully." And in spite of everything, the Supariwalas wanted to stay on. That was what amazed Ann. They came to her, cowering, crying, thundering, insulting—rehearsed or spontaneous—and still they found reasons for staying where Ann herself, on bad days, found few.

A little before eleven Bella brought over a small, mustached man in white shirt and bright blue suit, gold cuff-links, gold tie-bar, gold rings and a gold tooth. He'd recently lit a cigarette; he took two frenzied puffs before crushing it out.

"Annie, this is Mr. Hernandez. He has a problem but I told him I don't think we can help him."

He did not take a seat.

"Is it a Human Rights problem, Mr. Hernandez?"

He waved away the question. "I would not be here for anything less than Human Rights," he said.

She rolled paper into the typewriter, typed in the date, the time, and in the appropriate box, HERNANDEZ.

"Your first name, please."

"It is not for me. It is for my sister. You see, she came to Canada to join her new husband, but he's the big shot, see. He runs off to P.E.I. with another girl. What can she do? Her visitor's visa runs out in three days."

"Her husband now refuses to sponsor her?"

"Yes, yes, he wants now to marry that other girl."

"If she has no spouse to sponsor her, then she is in a difficult situation."

"That is what Immigration says. But I will sponsor her. I make good money. I sell houses all day. At night I am cosmetic salesman. What do they think? She is going to become a welfare mother with a dozen kids?"

She watched his thin body stiffen. It crossed her mind that Mr. Hernandez was a proud man, that the gold was in some way intended to publicize his importance, and that it might have succeeded in a different country. Such men were hard to deal with, they took Human Rights too literally. She would probably have to take a taxi to the Windsor Arms, instead of walking.

"Mr. Hernandez"—she flashed her most sympathetic smile as she unrolled the sheet of paper—"what you describe, I'm afraid, really is not a problem for Human Rights." She looked beyond him at the lobby where two more complainants sat alertly, one of them bandaged and clearly a candidate for her time. What to tell Mr. Hernandez? Buy a T-shirt and proclaim something defiant? Hire a caustic lawyer? The cuffs—too wide—were dingy; the collar wrinkled; it was a sign, Ann felt, that she'd been too long in the job. A long time ago, she had come early to work and stayed late and been greedy for piles of complaints to process. Each form, somehow, improving things just a little. She'd listened to other people's catastrophes and been drawn to their garish wardrobes, their inappropriate flatteries, their occasional threats, their faith in her power. At Miss Edgar's and Miss Cramp's she had been thought of as a selfless person because she talked of joining CUSO eventually. But she had not gone to New Guinea or Malawi. She had gone to McGill, then moved to Toronto. Her job had worn her down. She had tried too earnestly to correct the nation's wrongs. Now she saw problems only as a bureaucrat. Deal only with the sure things. Pass the others off. Get documentation. Promise nothing.

"Her name is Isabella," Mr. Hernandez said. "I can bring her in."

"That won't be necessary, Mr. Hernandez. Please. You must understand: Human Rights refers to a specific set of grievances. You must understand—"

She was thinking of the picture of Poppy in that morning's *Globe and Mail*. Poppy looked vulnerable in spite of all her sexiness. She remembered the leafy playgrounds of Westmount and Poppy leaning against her bicycle, peeling back kneesocks to show off what she called "kiss-wounds," where boys with teeth like penknives had paid their homage.

"What? Understand what?"

Now it's your turn, Annie. Come on, show me, don't be a spoil-sport. But Ann had nothing to show, then or now; at twenty-six her skin was still spongy white, impervious to damage.

Mr. Hernandez reached for her wrist across the cluttered desk and knocked aside a stack of dossiers. Ann was well brought up; she could not draw back her hand from the distasteful pressure of Mr. Hernandez's fingers. She let her wrist go limp in the warm funnel of his clutch. She knew she was safe; she could refer his case to a different department. She could afford to pat his hand, to smile, to assure him that Immigration would listen to his case. She sealed off the promise with another sympathetic smile.

After Mr. Hernandez left, she excused herself and took refuge in the staff-only toilet. She wore little make-up, and her face always looked edgy, only the bright red lipstick made people think the effect was contrived rather than accidental. She leaned against the wet, scarred counter and touched up the faded red, trying not to feel guilty about the men still waiting to be interviewed. Her wrist was warm and throbbing, as though wrapped in a tight, moist bandage. Mr. Hernandez, for a frail man, had left his mark.

With twenty minutes to go, she found herself typing PERSAWD, JOHN MOHAN. A subway assault. Queen Street Station this time: chipped teeth, cut lips, broken nose, blackened eyes. Cuts, abrasions. Persawd had brought a lawyer, or a law student, perhaps a relative, to press his grievance. Three months in Toronto, the lawyer was saying, and *this*. What kind of people are you? What kind of city is this?

"You have reported this to the police?" she asked.

"Of course, of course. But what good are the police? The assailants fled. We have no witnesses. The police suggest my client got drunk and started a fight, Miss Vane. They make this boy feel like a complainer. The victims are made to feel guilty."

I know, thought Ann. But what, exactly, could Human Rights do? What specific recommendation follows from this incident? She took down documentation, ages of the assailants, fodder for another Royal Commission. The Queen Street file was already thick, justification for permanent patrols? But no thicker than a dozen others. And Torontonians were proud of their subway, their politeness, proud of their moral spotlessness. This after all was not New York. Assaults on John Mohan Persawd and dozens like him would always be considered isolated incidents, and who's to say they were racial in nature? Police treated it as simple assault, rowdiness, and drew no necessary inferences regarding race. No witnesses, no case, and police involvement ended. And so she typed, entering facts, censoring opinions, absorbing a small human drama that had lost its power to touch her. What of my client's dignity? the lawyer asked. What of the boy who dreamed of coming to Canada? Who waited five years for immigration? Who trained as an electrician in Guyana but now washed windows?

"I have no answers for such questions," said Ann.

"It's time that you did, Miss Vane."

The snowy gleam of fluorescence helped; it stamped out feelings and faces, it miniaturized passions, like a television screen. Hand in hand with January, it helped her accept imperfections in the world, her own limitation. She had wanted to be a poet, and at one time she seemed closer to success in poetry than Poppy had in music. Poppy had sung, not badly, in a schoolgirl performance of *Brigadoon* and, like dozens of other Westmount girls, had sung in little clubs on Dorchester, then Stanley and Mountain. No one thought too much of her; just another aspiring Joni Mitchell, looking better than she sounded. But Ann had gone to McGill and won some prizes; she'd fantasized about expiring exquisitely like Sylvia Plath, leaving behind a poignant lyric or two. Then suddenly Poppy was in New York and they wrote her up in the *Gazette* as a hot new property. By the time Ann graduated, Poppy had become Peppi, folk had yielded to disco, and she'd dumped the Montreal boy who'd been guiding her career and had taken on a genius agent and business manager who ran her life like Prussian generals, according to *People*. And Aunt Nellie had died and Ann had bought herself a small, sturdy house on Tranby.

"Canadians are mean as hell," said John Mohan Persawd. "Life is hopeless, man, no justice, no redress."

"I don't know about that," said Ann. "If this had happened in New York, you'd have been left for dead."

"Correction, Miss Vane," said the lawyer. "If this had happened in New York, he'd have been mugged for his money, not racially assaulted."

On good days it would have seemed an academic distinction. Statistically, where would you rather be? Aesthetically, which subway would you prefer to ride? But on bad days, judgments curled up at her from a thousand scraps of paper and she could only tell herself that if all these recommendations, all this paperwork, all this good sense and reason were not influencing *something*, she would quit.

She had a hard time getting a cab. A young taxi-driver delivering a dozen giant, obscenely inscribed chocolate-chip cookies took pity on her, there in the cold without benefit of her trusty boots, and dropped her at the corner of St. Thomas and Bloor.

The hotel lobby was full of stout, tanned men in

denim suits, and of tall, tanned women glowing like oranges from too much California. All the faces seemed anonymously familiar: from soap operas, perhaps, or supporting roles in long-running series. They were here to star (she'd read somewhere) in some Canadian pornographic film. Ann had hoped Poppy would meet her in the lobby so she wouldn't have to pick her way through the thicket of self-possessed guests, but Poppy was still in her suite, just recently risen, sipping champagne, watching a game show and painting her nails.

Her public would not have recognized her. She was almost a tired-looking Poppy Pennington of Anwoth Drive. Ann thought of herself always looking the same: sensible, efficient, vaguely sporty. Poppy-Peppi had settled into at least two selves: one a ravishing seventeen (latest album, *Cream in Your Jeans*), the other a wispy thirty. Her voice was breathless, as though it now required amplification simply to be audible, as if it wouldn't be heard at all if she weren't belting it out. She didn't move from her chair—she indicated the wet, green nails—and her feet were up on the bed. But she radiated her oldest and warmest smile and said to Ann, "Have some champagne?"

A sideboard was stocked with liquor, with stacks of plastic glasses and bottles of mix. Ann poured herself a Dubonnet and topped it with ginger ale.

"You look wonderful," Ann said. "Different, of course, but wonderful."

The throaty laugh, the long cough, "You're as nice as ever. You don't have to say things like that, you know. I look like I belong on the Main—no, I look like the morning after a night on the Main. It's a punishment, Annie, getting up this early. It's this life—another album and I split. But you're the one who's looking wonderful. So *healthy*, Christ! So . . . *centered*, you know? How do you do it—men? Exercise, pills, a shrink, what?''

"Poppy, come on."

"They'd eat you alive in California, Annie. They haven't seen fresh meat in years out there—my God, you're actually blushing! A girl who can blush is worth her weight in gold or other substances, believe me. When I get off the road this time, you'll come out and visit me, promise, okay?''

Ann sipped the Dubonnet; with the ginger ale it looked as if she'd been too greedy. She gulped it quickly, then poured another, smaller, without the mix. She was unsure if lunch was to be sent up or eaten below in the Courtyard. Poppy looked at least an hour away from any public appearance, and Ann would have to be back, filing complaints by then. California! All the questions that Ann had prepared—anything she could say to such a wildly successful friend from her childhood—seemed suddenly giddy, or vaguely insulting, as though she were trying to whittle Poppy down to the level from which they'd both started.

"Tell me about Los Angeles," she begged. "Is it really . . . crazy?''

"Every place is crazy," Poppy teased. She slid a freshly-painted nail into her glass of Perrier and flicked pulp off the twist of lemon. "L.A.'s just crazier than most.''

She began to sketch, with relish, her life of apparent immorality. She described circular waterbeds, the mirrored ceilings (''They're glued like tiles, and I know one day a tile's going to fall and slice some guy's ass to pieces!''), the amyls given her by her last boyfriend, the parties she gave, the parties she had to go to to please her agent. She named some names, denied some others. Her kimono fell away, baring her sloping, blue-veined thighs. "I'm sick of sex, frankly," she said.

"I think I know what you mean," Ann ventured.

"I'm sure you do, I was admiring those marks on your wrist. Bondage? Oh, Annie, you've got that blush down *pat*. It's great!"

Ann was on her third Dubonnet; she'd forgotten the forceful entreaties of Mr. Hernandez, bless him. Poppy continued with the anecdotes. With bold, crude gestures she relived the saga of the resisting heart. Ann could still detect that old charm, the vulnerabilities of the prepubescent Westmount girl who had inflicted flesh wounds on her shins and calves to set herself apart from the comforting staidness of her surroundings. It should have been entirely predictable even then: she would leave in order to be able to return, again and again. The dour reasonableness of Canada would see to that. Who knew how flamboyant and crude Ann herself might have become if she had escaped on a Greyhound carrying a sleeping bag and *Beautiful Losers*? From the window, which was gritty with cold, she could make out the diners at the Courtyard. Poppy made no move to get dressed. There was little hope of eating now and being seen and still getting back to the office on time.

Every anecdote brought Ann down to the deep spongy core of her own failure. "You were a bit of a writer in school, weren't you, Annie?" Poppy said suddenly. She turned the TV off, snapping shut a middle-aged nurse who had won $876 worth of rattan furniture. "Tom Packer and you would get on famously. He's an old

Montrealer with connections. He can throw script-writing jobs your way. He fixes scripts that get botched. Very important work, if you don't mind not getting credit.''

"I wouldn't mind.'' She drifted in a speculative haze: still a poet, her poems remembered, but a freelancer too. She watched hours of television, she still read and went to movies; she probably wouldn't be bad. Every day at work she saw men and women who had sold their savings in tropical villages to make new beginnings in icy Canada. Not everyone had done well, but they had taken a chance. Sometimes you have to leave the safe and sober places of this world. She could learn to write scripts instead of poems, which she didn't write any-more anyway. Jokes and brilliant one-liners could punctuate improbable car chases. She wouldn't be responsible for the action scenes anyway, she thought. Poppy had shown her that you could come home again and again.

The Dubonnets were getting to her. Her face, she suspected, was already flushed (a hereditary flaw), though her deportment would remain respectable for another couple of hours. Poppy had taken over the bathroom. Her voice rose and fell over the splash of water and the whine of electrical gadgetry. She was telling Ann about Tom, how she absolutely adored him. He was building a yacht. He had worshipped Baba Ram Dass. He had played with Herb Alpert. He had once barbecued a rattler.

It was not Poppy, but Peppi Paluka who came out of the bathroom. She wore a leather vest without shirt or bra; even her forearms were sullenly sensuous. She was nearly the girl on the jacket of *Cream in Your Jeans*.

"I've got to get back to work," Ann said. She was a little frightened of this manifestation.

"I wish you could stay longer, but some people are coming up." Poppy sat on the coffee table and pulled on her boots. They were cowboy boots of bright baby blue, with purple, hand-tooled leaves and flowers.

"I thought of you all morning," Ann confessed. "I could hardly get any work done."

"Me too, Annie-poo. You've gotta come out and visit."

Ann promised, all too readily. In the spring, before Poppy's London opening, definitely. Poppy would arrange for her to meet everyone: Donald Sutherland, if he wasn't filming on an ice floe somewhere, would she like that? Margot Kidder, Tom Packer, anyone. They would gossip about home. They would careen down the canyons. They would cruise the beaches with Tom, once he worked out his sexual identity. The future would be even better than the past. In order to get her ready, Poppy rooted through the closet, opening sacks and boxes, taking out bright summertime T-shirts and open-toed, pastel shoes with high acrylic heels. "All the rage, Annie. Here, take what you want. I'll make you into a disco-mama. We'll have fun." She pressed Ann against her hard, slithery breasts, they brushed cheeks, and Ann—flushing and shivering—gathered her presents and left.

Ann stopped at a Colonel Sanders spot on Bloor for a quick snack-pack. The only other time she had eaten there had been with a girl from the office—Marie something—who had taken out half a dozen girls on the day she'd quit. She'd married an engineer and gone off to Zambia. "I'm afraid," she'd told Ann. "Toronto's the farthest I've been from Jonquière.'' But Ann had thought her fear a form of vanity, a way of showing off that her life was not closing in on her, as was the life of the more circumspect Ann Vane. Anyway, when you're from Jonquière, what fears can Africa hold? Coming to Toronto had been her training in foreign travel.

"What's there to be afraid of?" Ann had deflated her. "Guy'll be working for a Canadian company, won't he? You'll be living in a Canadian compound. You'll probably even have a Canadian PX.''

"The seasons come at the wrong time," Marie had said. "They don't have electricity all day. My things won't work there.''

Ann had no idea how it had turned out for the girl in Zambia. There had been no letters to anyone at the office, not even a Christmas card, though Ann had hunted up a *Joyeux Noël* and sent it to the engineering company in Lusaka. Africa had swallowed her. Now, as she sat at a table not far from teenagers wearing roller skates, the old irritations at Marie's confession returned. She, too, could leave if she wanted to. It wasn't fear or frugality that kept her back. She lacked ferocity of desire. That was her failing. She would think of going to L.A. to visit Poppy Pennington. Who knew, she might even try writing for Tom Packer. Home was a territory of the mind; it was altogether possible she would call up one of the dozens of real-estate agents who dropped cards in her mailbox and put the house on Tranby up for sale. She'd make a killing.

"Miss Vane, excuse me, please, may I bother you? You have one minute?''

She cringed. The man—it was Mr. Hernandez, this

time in an overcoat that muted his dingy flamboyance—had been sitting a few tables away and must have been studying her, waiting for the moment (her thoughts of California? of selling her house? had she been moving her lips?) to pounce. But why would he drag over his tray and briefcase?

"It's my lunch hour," she said stiffly. She had not meant to humiliate him. She had not meant to stop at a fast-food place. She had meant to be dining in the famous Courtyard Cafe with Peppi Paluka.

"You have a moment for someone in pain?" He stood before her, accusatory, penitential, the briefcase wedged upright between his tireless legs.

"You see that lady there." He didn't point, and she did not lift her head, or smile. "She wants to meet you, Miss Vane. That is my sister. She says you understand melancholia. She talks to you, woman to woman—I am going away. She says you know the pain in her heart, you will help. You will let her stay."

Please, thought Ann, *enough*. She wasn't good with melodrama, with passionate delivery that sounded like bad translation. "I told you," she said, "it is not my department. I have nothing to do with visas." She would not permit him to wheedle away her resistance. She knew nothing about love, though she had been betrayed once. Her man in condo development, who had brought her pale, pretty bottles of wine, who'd flown her once to Florida, who'd pinned her indiscriminately against refrigerator doors, in closets, on sofas and guest beds, in a burlesque of uncontainable passion. It had been a mistake, and after he had wounded her vanity she had returned to work as usual, slowed just a little by Bella's Valium. She thought Mr. Hernandez, who'd left his marks on her wrist, who sold houses and cosmetics, capable of the same behavior. She had not done what she had wanted to—put her head in an oven like Sylvia Plath—and she would not do whatever Mr. Hernandez wanted now. She had been, and would be, sensible and brave.

"You will not let her be deported. Please." He reached for her arm, which she skillfully withdrew. "You see how crazy she is with devotion. She *will* find her husband. I will go and talk reason. Then she will take the bus to P.E.I."

"*Mister* Hernandez, please. Kindly leave me alone, have I made myself clear? I'm going on vacation soon. You could try talking to Mrs. Herzog. She'll take over my cases. But I hold out little hope for your sister. The law is quite inflexible on that point."

"It's not fair," Mr. Hernandez shouted. "You cannot leave us like . . . like dogs on the street."

To keep him from shouting, from making a scene in a room full of roller skaters, she was forced to look up. He was a madman. He pushed his briefcase toward her with angry, shuffling steps. His breathing was unsteady, full of clucking and rattling noises. He thrust his ungloved hands at her in a petition so savage that she was afraid he might kill her. His fingers were flat and bony under the too-short sleeves of his coat. They came at her, like knife blades, to gouge and slice her face.

"Go away," she cried. "Tell your sister to go back. They'll find her and arrest her if she overstays."

He withdrew. "You promised to work something out," he said, plaintively. "My poor sister, now she goes mad, she kills herself, who knows? She has too much pain. But don't worry. I don't want you to worry,

Miss Vane. You're free to finish your food and look at all the nice clothes you bought from all the nice shops. I don't want to give you stomach ache or worse. You people cannot feel, that is the problem.''

She hated him. If only she could think of something wounding enough to say. ''That's preposterous. Absolutely preposterous.'' But he was already walking away, his back sternly discouraging of second thoughts, second chances. ''Nothing is fair!'' she shouted, ashamed at letting go like that, in a public place. ''You think I have it good?''

She watched him fade into the wintry crowd. The woman he'd pointed to did not jump up, did not even take notice. Wherever the sister was, she would not go mad or jump out of a window and splatter herself on downtown traffic as Ann had dreamed of, often. Mr. Hernandez's sister would hide in back rooms with drapes pulled tight, crouch behind the sofa at each ring of the doorbell, stare at game shows till glassy-eyed. She would not get caught. She would not be deported. She wasn't ambitious enough to get deeply hurt.

''Nothing is fair!'' she shouted. ''There isn't any justice. And your sister was never married! It's a trick to cheat Immigration.'' Her voice sagged with grief, and she sat, a small figure at the end of a long, busy dining hall. She would not stand in line with Donald Sutherland, not Ann; she would remain in Toronto surrounded by Chinese and Indians and Jamaicans, bent over their snack-packs of Kentucky Fried Chicken.

After a while, they stopped staring. Ann gathered up her presents and walked back to the office.

Nostalgia

ON a cold, snowless evening in December, Dr. Manny Patel, a psychiatric resident at a state hospital in Queens, New York, looked through the storefront window of the "New Taj Mahal" and for the first time in thirteen years felt the papercut-sharp pain of desire. The woman behind the counter was about twenty, twenty-one, with the buttery-gold skin and the round voluptuous bosom of a Bombay film star.

Dr. Patel had driven into Manhattan on an impulse. He had put in one of those afternoons at the hospital that made him realize it was only the mysteries of metabolism that kept him from unprofessional outbursts. Mr. Horowitz, a 319-pound readmitted schizophrenic, had convinced himself that he was Noel Coward and demanded respect from the staff. In less than half an hour, Mr. Horowitz had sung twenty songs, battered a therapy aide's head against a wall, unbuttoned another patient's blouse in order to bite off her nipples, struck a Jamaican nurse across the face and lunged at Dr. Patel, calling him in exquisite English, "Paki scum." The

nurse asked that Mr. Horowitz be placed in the seclusion room, and Dr. Patel had agreed. The seclusion
order had to be reviewed by a doctor every two hours,
and Mr. Horowitz's order was renewed by Dr. Chuong
who had come in two hours late for work.

Dr. Patel did not like to lock grown men and women
in a seven-by-nine room, especially one without pad-
ding on its walls. Mr. Horowitz had screamed and sung
for almost six hours. Dr. Patel had increased his dosage
of Haldol. Mr. Horowitz was at war with himself and
there was no truce except through psychopharmacology
and Dr. Patel was suspicious of the side effects of such
cures. The Haldol had calmed the prisoner. Perhaps it
was unrealistic to want more.

He was grateful that there were so many helpless,
mentally disabled people (crazies, his wife called them)
in New York state, and that they afforded him and Dr.
Chuong and even the Jamaican nurse a nice living. But
he resented being called a "Paki scum." Not even a
sick man like Mr. Horowitz had the right to do that.

He had chosen to settle in the U.S. He was not one
for nostalgia; he was not an expatriate but a patriot. His
wife, Camille, who had grown up in Camden, New
Jersey, did not share his enthusiasm for America, and
had made fun of him when he voted for President Rea-
gan. Camille was not a hypocrite; she was a predictable
paradox. She could cut him down for wanting to move
to a three-hundred-thousand-dollar house with an atrium
in the dining hall, and for blowing sixty-two thousand
on a red Porsche, while she boycotted South African
wines and non-union lettuce. She spent guiltless money
at Balducci's and on fitness equipment. So he enjoyed
his house, his car, so what? He wanted things. He

wanted things for Camille and for their son. He loved his family, and his acquisitiveness was entwined with love.

His son was at Andover, costing nearly twelve thousand dollars a year. When Manny converted the twelve thousand from dollars to rupees, which he often did as he sat in his small, dreary office listening for screams in the hall, the staggering rupee figure reassured him that he had done well in the New World. His son had recently taken to wearing a safety pin through his left earlobe, but nothing the boy could do would diminish his father love.

He had come to America because of the boy. Well, not exactly *come*, but stayed when his student visa expired. He had met Camille, a nurse, at a teaching hospital and the boy had come along, all eight pounds and ten ounces of him, one balmy summer midnight. He could always go back to Delhi if he wanted to. He had made enough money to retire to India (the conversion into rupees had made him a millionaire several times over). He had bought a condominium in one of the better development "colonies" of New Delhi, just in case.

America had been very good to him, no question; but there were things that he had given up. There were some boyhood emotions, for instance, that he could no longer retrieve. He lived with the fear that his father would die before he could free himself from the crazies of New York and go home. He missed his parents, especially his father, but he couldn't explain this loss to Camille. She hated her mother who had worked long hours at Korvette's and brought her up alone. Camille's mother now worked at a K-Mart, even though she didn't need the money desperately. Camille's mother was an obsessive-compulsive but that was no reason to hate her. In fact, Manny got along with her very well and often had to carry notes between her and her daughter.

His father was now in his seventies, a loud, brash man with blackened teeth. He still operated the moviehouse he owned. The old man didn't trust the manager he kept on the payroll. He didn't trust anyone except his blood relatives. All the ushers in the moviehouse were poor cousins. Manny was an only child. His mother had been deemed barren, but at age forty-three, goddess Parvati had worked a miracle and Manny had been born. He should go back to India. He should look after his parents. Out of a sense of duty to the goddess, if not out of love for his father. Money, luxuries; he could have both in India, too. When he had wanted to go to Johns Hopkins for medical training, his parents had loved him enough to let him go. They loved him the same intense, unexamined way he loved his own boy. He had let them down. Perhaps he hadn't really let them down in that he had done well at medical school, and had a job in the State set-up in Queens, and played the money market aggressively with a bit of inside information from Suresh Khanna who had been a year ahead of him in Delhi's Modern School and was now with Merrill-Lynch, but he hadn't reciprocated their devotion.

It was in this mood of regret filtered through longing that Manny had driven into Manhattan and parked his Porsche on a sidestreet outside the Sari Palace which was a block up from the New Taj Mahal, where behind the counter he had spied the girl of his dreams.

The girl—the woman, Manny corrected himself instantly, for Camille didn't tolerate what she called "masculists"—moved out from behind the counter to show a customer where in the crowded store the ten-pound bags of Basmati rice were stacked. She wore a "Police" T-shirt and navy cords. The cords voluted up her small, rounded thighs and creased around her crotch in a delicate burst, like a Japanese fan. He would have dressed her in a sari of peacock blue silk. He wanted to wrap her narrow wrists in bracelets of 24-carat gold. He wanted to decorate her bosom and throat with neck-laces of pearls, rubies, emeralds. She was as lovely and as removed from him as a goddess. He breathed warm, worshipful stains on the dingy store window.

She stooped to pick up a sack of rice by its rough jute handles while the customer flitted across the floor to a bin of eggplants. He discerned a touch of indolence in the way she paused before slipping her snake-slim fingers through the sack's hemp loops. She paused again. She tested the strength of the loops. She bent her knees, ready to heave the brutish sack of rice. He found himself running into the store. He couldn't let her do it. He couldn't let a goddess do menial chores, then ride home on a subway with a backache.

"Oh, thank you," she said. She flashed him an in-dolent glance from under heavily shadowed eyelids, without seeming to turn away from the customer who had expected her to lift the ten-pound sack.

"Where are the fresh eggplants? These are all dried out."

Manny Patel watched the customer flick the pleats of her Japanese georgette sari irritably over the sturdy tops of her winter boots.

"These things look as if they've been here all week!" the woman continued to complain.

Manny couldn't bear her beauty. Perfect crimson nails raked the top layer of eggplant. "They came in just two days ago."

If there had been room for a third pair of hands, he would have come up with plump, seedless, perfect eggplants.

"Ring up the rice, *dal* and spices," the customer instructed. "I'll get my vegetables next door."

"I'll take four eggplants," Manny Patel said defiantly. "And two pounds of *bhindi*." He sorted through wilted piles of okra which Camille wouldn't know how to cook.

"I'll be with you in a minute, sir," the goddess answered.

When she looked up again, he asked her out for dinner. She said only, "You really don't have to buy anything, you know."

She suggested they meet outside the Sari Palace at six-thirty. Her readiness overwhelmed him. Dr. Patel had been out of the business of dating for almost thirteen years. At conferences, on trips and on the occasional night in the city when an older self possessed him, he would hire women for the evening, much as he had done in India. They were never precisely the answer, not even to his desire.

Camille had taken charge as soon as she had spotted him in the hospital cafeteria; she had done the pursuing. While he did occasionally flirt with a Filipino nutritionist at the hospital where he now worked, he assumed he did not possess the dexterity to perform the two-step dance of assertiveness and humility required of serious adultery. He left the store flattered, but wary. A goddess had found him attractive, but he didn't know her name. He didn't know what kind of family fury she might unleash on him. Still, for the first time in years he felt a kind of agitated discovery, as though if he let up for a minute, his reconstituted, instant American life would not let him back.

His other self, the sober, greedy, scholarly Dr. Patel, knew that life didn't change that easily. He had seen enough Horowitzes to know that no matter how astute his own methods might be and no matter how miraculous the discoveries of psychopharmacologists, fate could not be derailed. How did it come about that Mr. Horowitz, the son of a successful slacks manufacturer, a good student at the Bronx High School of Science, had ended up obese, disturbed and assaultive, while he, the son of a Gujarati farmer turned entrepreneur, an indifferent student at Modern School and then at St. Stephen's in Delhi, was ambitious and acquisitive? All his learning and experience could not answer the simplest questions. He had about an hour and twenty minutes to kill before perfection was to revisit him, this time (he guessed) in full glory.

Dr. Patel wandered through "little India"—the busy, colorful blocks of Indian shops and restaurants off Lexington in the upper twenties. Men lugged heavy crates out of doubleparked pickup trucks, swearing in Punjabi and Hindi. Women with tired, frightened eyes stepped into restaurants, careful not to drop their shopping sacks from Bloomingdale's and Macy's. The Manhattan air here was fragrant with spices. He followed an attractive mother with two preschoolers into Chadni Chowk, a tea and snacks stall, to call Camille about the emergency that had come up. Thank God for Mr. Horowitz's recidivism. Camille was familiar with the more outrageous doings of Mr. Horowitz.

"Why does that man always act up when I have plans?" Camille demanded. "*Amarcord* is at the rep tonight only."

But Camille seemed in as agreeable a mood as his goddess. She thought she might ask Susan Kwan, the wife of an orthodontist who lived four houses up the block and who had a son by a former marriage also at Andover. Her credulousness depressed Manny. A woman who had lived with a man for almost thirteen years should be able to catch his little lies.

"Mr. Horowitz is a dangerous person," he continued. He could have hung up, but he didn't. He didn't want permission; he wanted sympathy. "He rushed into my office. He tried to kill me."

"Maybe psychiatrists at state institutions ought to carry firearms. Have you thought of that, Manny?" She laughed.

Manny Patel flushed. Camille didn't understand how the job was draining him. Mr. Horowitz had, for a fact, flopped like a walrus on Dr. Patel's desk, demanding a press conference so that the world would know that his civil liberties were being infringed. The moneyless schizos of New York state, Mr. Horowitz had screamed, were being held hostage by a bunch of foreign doctors who couldn't speak English. If it hadn't been for the two six-foot orderlies (Dr. Patel felt an awakening of respect for big blacks), Mr. Horowitz would probably have grabbed him by the throat.

"I could have died today," he repeated. The realization dazed him. "The man tried to strangle me."

He hung up and ordered a cup of masala tea. The

sweet, sticky brew calmed him, and the perfumed steam
cleared his sinuses. Another man in his position would
probably have ordered a double scotch. In crises, he
seemed to regress, to reach automatically for the miracle cures of his Delhi youth, though normally he had
no patience with nostalgia. When he had married, he
burned his India Society membership card. He was pro-
fessionally cordial, nothing more, with Indian doctors
at the hospital. But he knew he would forever shuttle
between the old world and the new. He couldn't pretend
he had been reborn when he became an American citizen in a Manhattan courthouse. Rebirth was the priv-
ilege of the dead, and of gods and goddesses, and they
could leap into your life in myriad, mysterious ways, as
a shopgirl, for instance, or as a withered eggplant, just
to test you.

At three minutes after six, Dr. Patel positioned himself inside his Porsche and watched the front doors of
the Sari Palace for his date's arrival. He didn't want to
be late, but more than that he didn't want to give the
appearance of having been early, or of having waited
nervously. There was a slight tremor in both his hands.
He was suffering a small attack of anxiety. At thirty-
three minutes after six, she appeared in the doorway
of the sari store. She came out of the Sari Palace, not up
the street from the New Taj Mahal as he had expected.
He slammed shut and locked his car door. Did it mean
that she too had come to the rendezvous too early and
had spied on him, crouched, anxious, strapped in the
bucket seat of his Porsche? When he caught up with her
by the store window, she was the most beautiful woman
he had ever talked to.

Her name was Padma. She told him that as he fought

for a cab to take them uptown. He didn't ask for, and she didn't reveal, her last name. Both were aware of the illicit nature of their meeting. An Indian man his age had to be married, though he wore no wedding ring. An immigrant girl from a decent Hindu family— it didn't matter how long she had lived in America and what rock groups she was crazy about—would not have said yes to dinner with a man she didn't know. It was this inarticulated unsanctionedness of the dinner date that made him feel reckless, a hedonist, a man who might trample tired ladies carrying shopping bags in order to steal a taxi crawling uptown. He wanted to take Padma to an Indian restaurant so that he would feel he knew what he was ordering and could bully the maitre d' a bit, but not to an Indian restaurant in her neighborhood. He wanted a nice Indian restaurant, an upscale one, with tablecloths, sitar music and air ducts sprayed with the essence of rose petals. He chose a new one, Shajahan, on Park Avenue.

"It's nice. I was going to recommend it," she said.

Padma. Lotus. The goddess had come to him as a flower. He wanted to lunge for her hands as soon as they had been seated at a corner booth, but he knew better than to frighten her off. He was mortal, he was humble.

The maitre d' himself took Dr. Patel's order. And with the hors d'oeuvres of samosas and poppadoms he sent a bottle of Entre Deux Mers on the house. Dr. Patel had dined at the Shajahan four or five times already, and each time had brought in a group of six or eight. He had been a little afraid that the maitre d' might disapprove of his bringing a youngish woman, an

Indian and quite obviously not his wife, but the bottle of wine reassured him that the management was not judgmental.

He broke off a sliver of poppadom and held it to her lips. She snatched it with an exaggerated flurry of lips and teeth.

"Feeding the performing seal, are you?" She was coy. And amused.

"I didn't mean it that way," he murmured. Her lips, he noticed, had left a glistening crescent of lipstick on a fingertip. He wiped the finger with his napkin surreptitiously under the table.

She didn't help herself to the sarmosas, and he didn't dare lift a forkful to her mouth. Perhaps she didn't care for samosas. Perhaps she wasn't much of an eater. He himself was timid and clumsy, half afraid that if he tried anything playful he might drip mint chutney on her tiger-print chiffon sari.

"Do you mind if I smoke?"

He busied himself with food while she took out a packet of Sobrani and a book of matches. Camille had given up smoking four years before, and now hand-written instructions THANK YOU FOR NOT SMOKING IN THIS HOUSE decorated bureau tops and coffee tables. He had never gotten started because of an allergy.

"Well?" she said. It wasn't quite a question, and it wasn't quite a demand. "Aren't you going to light it?" And she offered Manny Patel an exquisite profile, cheek sucked tight and lips squeezed around the filter tip.

The most banal gesture of a goddess can destroy a decent-living mortal. He lit her cigarette, then blew the match out with a gust of unreasonable hope.

The maitre d' hung around Manny's table almost to the point of neglecting other early diners. He had sad eyes and a bushy mustache. He wore a dark suit, a silvery wide tie kept in place with an elephant-headed god stick pin, and on his feet which were remarkably large for a short, slight man, scuffed and pointed black shoes.

"I wouldn't recommend the pork vindaloo tonight." The man's voice was confidential, low. "We have a substitute cook. But the fish Bengal curry is very good. The lady, I think, is Bengali, no?"

She did not seem surprised. "How very observant of you, sir," she smiled.

It was flattering to have the maitre d' linger and advise. Manny Patel ended up ordering one each of the curries listed under beef, lamb and fowl. He was a guiltlessly meat-eating Gujarati, at least in America. He filled in the rest of the order with two vegetable dishes, one spiced lentil and a vegetable pillau. The raita salad was free, as were the two small jars of mango and lemon pickle.

When the food started coming, Padma reluctantly stubbed out her Sobrani. The maitre d' served them himself, making clucking noises with his tongue against uneven, oversize teeth, and Dr. Patel felt obliged to make loud, appreciative moans.

"Is everything fine, doctor-*sahib*? Fish is first class, no? It is not on the regular menu."

He stayed and made small talk about Americans. He dispatched waiters to other tables, directing them with claps of pinkish palms from the edge of Manny's booth. Padma made an initial show of picking at her vegetable pillau. Then she gave up and took out another slim black

Sobrani from a tin packet and held her face, uplifted and radiant, close to Manny's so he could light it again for her.

The maitre d' said, "I am having a small problem, doctor-*sahib*. Actually the problem is my wife's. She has been in America three years and she is very lonely still. I'm saying to her, you have nice apartment in Rego Park, you have nice furnitures and fridge and stove, I'm driving you here and there in a blue Buick, you're having home-style Indian food, what then is wrong? But I am knowing and you are knowing, doctor-*sahib*, that no Indian lady is happy without having children to bring up. That is why, in my desperation, I brought over my sister's child last June. We want to adopt him, he is very bright and talented and already he is loving this country. But the U.S. government is telling me no. The boy came on a visitor's visa, and now the government is giving me big trouble. They are calling me bad names. Jealous peoples are telling them bad stories. They are saying I'm in the business of moving illegal aliens, can you believe? In the meantime, my wife is crying all day and pulling out her hair. Doctor-*sahib*, you can write that she needs to have the boy here for her peace of mind and mental stability, no? On official stationery of your hospital, doctor-*sahib*?"

"My hands are tied," Manny Patel said. "The U.S. government wouldn't listen to me."

Padma said nothing. Manny ignored the maitre d'. A reality was dawning on Manny Patel. It was too beautiful, too exciting to contemplate. He didn't want this night to fall under the pressure of other immigrants' woes.

"But you will write a letter about my wife's mental

problems, doctor-*sahib*?'' The maitre d' had summoned up tears. A man in a dark suit weeping in an upscale ethnic restaurant. Manny felt slightly disgraced, he wished the man would go away. "Official stationery is very necessary to impress the immigration people."

"Please leave us alone," snapped Manny Patel. "If you persist I will never come back."

The old assurance, the authority of a millionaire in his native culture, was returning. He was sure of himself.

"What do you want to do after dinner?" Padma asked when the maitre d' scurried away from their booth. Manny could sense him, wounded and scowling, from behind the kitchen door.

"What would you like to do?" He thought of his wife and Mrs. Kwan at the Fellini movie. They would probably have a drink at a bar before coming home. Susan Kwan had delightful legs. He had trouble understanding her husband, but Manny Patel had spent enjoyable hours at the Kwans', watching Mrs. Kwans' legs. Padma's legs remained a mystery; he had seen her only in pants or a sari.

"If you are thinking of fucking me," she said very suddenly, "I should warn you that I never have an orgasm. You won't have to worry about pleasing me."

Yes, he thought, it *is* so, just as he had suspected. It was a night in which he could do no wrong. He waved his Visa card at the surly maitre d' and paid the bill. After that Padma let him take her elbow and guide her to the expensive hotel above the restaurant.

An oriental man at the desk asked him, "Cash or credit card, sir?" He paid for a double occupancy room

with cash and signed himself in as Dr. Mohan Vakil &
wife, 18 Ridgewood Drive, Columbus, Ohio.

He had laid claim to America.

In a dark seventh-floor room off a back corridor, the
goddess bared her flesh to a dazed, daunted mortal. She
was small. She was perfect. She had saucy breasts,
fluted thighs and tiny, taut big tocs.

"Hey, you can suck but don't bite, okay?" Padma
may have been slow to come, but he was not. He fell
on her with a devotee's frenzy.

"Does it bother you?" she asked later, smoking the
second Sobrani. She was on her side. Her tummy had a
hint of convex opulence. "About my not getting off?"

He couldn't answer. It was a small price to pay, and
anyway, he wasn't paying it. Nothing could diminish
the thrill he felt in taking a chance. It wasn't the hotel
and this bed; it was having stepped inside the New Taj
Mahal and asking her out.

He should probably call home, in case Camille hadn't
stopped off for a drink. He should probably get dressed,
offer her something generous—as discreetly as possible,
for this one had class, real class—then drive himself
home. The Indian food, an Indian woman in bed, made
him nostalgic. He wished he were in his kitchen, and
that his parents were visiting him and that his mother
was making him a mug of hot Horlick's and that his
son was not so far removed from him in a boarding
school.

He wished he had married an Indian woman. One
that his father had selected. He wished he had any life
but the one he had chosen.

As Dr. Patel sat on the edge of the double bed and
slid his feet through the legs of his trousers, someone

rapped softly on the hotel door, then without waiting for an answer unlocked it with a passkey.

Padma pulled the sheet up to her chin, but did not seem to have been startled.

"She's underage, of course," the maitre d' said. "She is my sister's youngest daughter. I accuse you of rape, doctor-*sahib*. You are of course ruined in this country. You have everything and think you must have more. You are highly immoral."

He sat on the one chair that wasn't littered with urgently cast-off clothes, and lit a cigarette. It was rapidly becoming stuffy in the room, and Manny's eyes were running. The man's eyes were malevolent, but the rest of his face remained practised and relaxed. An uncle should have been angrier, Dr. Patel thought automatically. He himself should have seen it coming. He had mistaken her independence as a bold sign of honest assimilation. But it was his son who was the traveller over shifting sands, not her.

There was no point in hurrying. Meticulously he put on his trousers, double-checked the zipper, buttoned his shirt, knotted his tie and slipped on his Gucci shoes. *The lady is Bengali, no?* Yes, they knew one another, perhaps even as uncle and niece. Or pimp and hooker. The air here was polluted with criminality. He wondered if his slacks had been made by immigrant women in Mr. Horowitz's father's sweatshop.

"She's got to be at least twenty-three, twenty-four," Dr. Patel said. He stared at her, deliberately insolent. Through the sheets he could make out the upward thrust of her taut big toes. He had kissed those toes only half an hour before. He must have been mad.

"I'm telling you she is a minor. I'm intending to

make a citizen's arrest. I have her passport in my pocket.''

It took an hour of bickering and threats to settle. He made out a check for seven hundred dollars. He would write a letter on hospital stationery. The uncle made assurances that there were no hidden tapes. Padma went into the bathroom to wash up and dress.

"Why?" Manny shouted, but he knew Padma couldn't hear him over the noise of the gushing faucet.

After the team left him, Manny Patel took off his clothes and went into the bathroom so recently used by the best-looking woman he had ever talked to (or slept with, he could now add). Her perfume, he thought of it as essence of lotus, made him choke.

He pulled himself up, using the edge of the bathtub as a step ladder, until his feet were on the wide edges of the old-fashioned sink. Then, squatting like a villager, squatting the way he had done in his father's home, he defecated into the sink, and with handfuls of his own shit—it felt hot, light, porous, an artist's medium—he wrote WHORE on the mirror and floor.

He spent the night in the hotel room. Just before dawn he took a cab to the parking lot of the Sari Palace. Miraculously, no vandals had touched his Porsche. Feeling lucky, spared somehow in spite of his brush with the deities, he drove home.

Camille had left the porch light on and it glowed pale in the brightening light of the morning. In a few hours Mr. Horowitz would start to respond to the increased dosage of Haldol and be let out of the seclusion chamber. At the end of the term, Shawn Patel would come home from Andover and spend all day in the house with earphones tuned to a happier world. And in August, he would take his wife on a cruise through the Caribbean and make up for this night with a second honeymoon.

Tamurlane

W E sleep in shifts in my apartment, three illegals on guard playing cards and three bedded down on mats on the floor. One man next door broke his leg jumping out the window. I'd been whistling in the bathroom and he'd mistaken it for our warning tune. The walls are flimsy. Nights I hear collective misery.

Was this what I left Ludhiana for?

It was below freezing and icy outside but inside the Mumtaz Bar B-Q it was hot and crackly with static. Mohan the busboy was gobbling the mints by the cash register. The cook was asleep on the bar's counter in his undershirt and shorts. He's a little guy and he can squeeze into the skinniest space, come three o'clock, or during a raid. The door is locked and the drapes are pulled. We have a "CLOSED" sign in English and Hindi on the door, courtesy of Cinema Sahni, next door. Mr. Aziz doesn't mind our spreading out of the kitchen and into the dining room as long as we spray air freshener before the dinner crowd comes in. These days Mr. A.

is dividing his time between the Mumtaz in Toronto and a 67-unit motel on the Gulf coast of Florida. Canadians don't want us, it's like Uganda all over again, says Mr. A. He says he can feel it in his bones.

So there we were, the regulars. The new tandoor chef, Gupta, was at a table with a huffing and puffing gentleman I didn't know. He had the crafty eyes of a Sindhi, but his graying hair was dyed reddish so he could have been a Muslim. I've been too long here; there was a time when I could tell them all apart, not just Hindu and Muslim, but where, what caste and what they were hiding. Now all I care about is legal or illegal? This man has called himself Muslim, a Ugandan, a victim of Idi Amin. These sad rehearsals, heaping indignity on top of being poor. As if poverty and opportunity weren't enough, like it was for the Italians and Greeks and Portuguese. How did this vast country suddenly get so filled? But Mr. A. and this chap probably have their British passports and their tales of mistreatment, and the rest of us have a lifetime debt to a shifty agent in Delhi who got us here, with no hint of how to keep us. The new chef and his friend made Mohan and me watchful.

He didn't have an old man's harassed face. His skin was oily still, and supple. He didn't look old enough to need to dye his hair. Vanity we're all guilty of; even the cook dropped a hundred and fifty dollars this December on hand-tooled, baby blue antelope boots. This man didn't look vain. He just seemed troubled. He held his cigarette Indian-style, high up near the glowing tip and in between the thumb and index finger, like a pencil.

I hadn't made up my mind about the new chef. He was a good chef, but an improviser. We didn't have an authentic tandoor oven because Mr. A. thinks people get bored of watching their meat cooked in a clay oven in front of them and if you aren't going to do the tandoor in public you might as well go down to Buffalo and buy one of the small, sturdy brick things from Khanna & Sons. We don't have one of the brick things either, not yet, but the new chef was doing wonders with chicken breasts and lamb chops under the broiler of our old gas stove. He didn't complain when he saw the Mumtaz's kitchen. He didn't say anything about the stove. He just limped into the freezer and took out two trays of lamb and chicken. Then he asked me where the cleaver was. But he wasn't friendly. He didn't want to talk. He walked like a man on unbending but fragile stilts. His knees didn't bend and when he sat his legs fell straight out. When he worked in the kitchen, he propped his stomach against the sink in order to keep his balance. Severe damage like that is difficult to watch, you want to pull away, as from a beggar.

Now he was doing the listening, and the man with the dyed hair was doing the talking.

The man said, "Maharaj, I don't know why you stay in Toronto, I really don't. I can find you a place in Atlanta, no immigration problems. Have you seen Atlanta in January? It's like a hill station, my friend. Like Simla, healthy. Or Dallas, here, let me check—" he took out a long list of names written on the back of a supermarket stub. "Ft. Worth, you are knowing?"

"Hey, man," Mohan called from the cash register, "you got a place for me on that list? I want New York City. Or Miami, hot-hot like Bombay."

"Pah, in Miami and New York they are finding thousands of boys like you. Big mouth and no skill. Don't bother me, I am talking to an artist with fish and fowl. Such a man is worth gold.''

The man put a hand on the new chef's hands which were folded and still, and red with tandoori masala in the knuckles and under the nails. The new chef didn't move. He looked dead, or very relaxed. I couldn't make up my mind about him. He was odd.

''If you stay here, trouble's going to find you. I can guarantee you that, my friend. Aziz-*sahib* has the right idea. Get out while you can. You're one of the lucky ones.''

Mohan rang the cash register. The drawer shot open and he took out a couple of quarters and fed them into the juke box. A noisy little number by a British group, and a duet by Chitra and Ajit Kumar.

The agent said nothing during the singles. When the music stopped, he said in the same hectoring tone he had used before, ''You don't have to go looking, friend. Because trouble's coming. If you stay in Toronto, it's coming to your door. You know what happened to me when I was coming to see you? Right here on Gerrard Street, a block and a half from your fancy Bar B-Q?''

Mohan didn't like the man. I could tell that from the way he kept trying to disrupt his story. He thought the man was giving the chef a hard time when all he wanted was a rest and smoke before his next shift. Mohan said, not loud but loud enough for me to hear and I was farther from him than the man was, ''This place isn't fancy. Mr. A. is a tightwad. Mr. A. couldn't run a fancy place.''

The recruiter didn't even look Mohan's way. He said, ''I was walking as fast as I could so we'd have time together before you had to cook again. You know how fast I can walk. You remember the time I was running to catch that train from Grand Central and I was stopped by a cop? He thought I was Puerto Rican, remember, because he had never seen an Indian run before. Well, I wasn't walking that fast, but fast, after getting off the trolley at the wrong stop. It was like that time we got off in the middle of Harlem—remember? I could see all the Indian shops up ahead, but I was still two blocks away. I started running, when out pop three young chaps from an arcade . . ."

"That must be Sinbad's," Mohan said. "The other arcade's four blocks the other side."

"One boy knocked me down. Actually he tripped me, so it looked like an accident. Then the other two spat on me, called me names you wouldn't believe. I'm a Gandhian of the old school. I just lay there with my face against a parking meter, to protect my eyes, you know. The eyes are delicate, the rest is reparable. And all the time the hooligans were belaboring me, my friend, I was thinking of you. Why did Gupta come back to Toronto, I kept asking. You were out once—I can get you back. I would be proud to sponsor a hero like you. I am proud to call you brother or cousin. You can pay me back a little every month—you'll be free in a year. Why, after what happened to you?" He turned now to Mohan, and there was scorn in his voice. "This man is a hero to us all. Six years ago when you were naked in Bombay, he was thrown on the subway tracks in this city. He would never walk, they said. Now look. Like a true Gandhian, he forgave them. Good men left Canada for less cause. Dr. Choudhury, he left his seventy-thousand-dollar-plus practice. On a matter of principle, you remember, when the courts let go those boys who beat up the worshippers at the Durga Puja festival.''

''Poor Dr. Choudhury,'' Mohan said to me. Principles are easy to have when you're rich and have a skill like Dr. Choudhury and Dallas is waiting. The problem is for Mohan and me and the little cook asleep on the bar. Hooligans and everyone else can do what they want and they know we don't dare complain.

''Why, my friend?'' The man put out his cigarette. ''What kind of a life is this if your dignity is on the line every time you step out the door?'' Ah, dignity. *Dignity!* that beautiful word that has never fed an empty stomach.

The chef just shrugged, but Mohan wasn't finished. He shouted, ''It's worse in British Columbia, except that the Sikhs can look after themselves better than we can. They go head-to-head with everyone. Thick skulls can be very useful.''

At four-thirty, the cook woke up and put away his pillow. The tandoor chef said goodbye to his friend, and walked back to his pans of marinating breasts and chops. The man said he was going back to Buffalo that night. Mohan was busier than the rest of us at any given hour. As a waiter I had it easiest. But it was lonely when the others went about their chores in the kitchen and I'd already folded the napkins into fancy shapes and laid the blue overcloths on the wobbly tables. Mr. A. had been gone so long to the Gulf coast that he didn't know the cook stole supplies and that I had become very bored. The Indian patrons came only on nights Sahni-*sahib* screened a Bombay blockbuster in the cinema next door. The white Canadians barely came at all. Maybe some old English types, or Indian boys with Canadian girlfriends, trying to show off. I don't know why our food never caught on with Canadians the way Chinese food did. We kept waiting for a notice in the papers, something like that. Mr. A. has a bigger place than this in Ft. Myers. Light of India or Star of India, something like that. He said he wanted to get into the take-out roti kabab business. "They'll be eating roti kababs the way they do hamburgers by the time I'm through," he used to brag. "I want to be the McDonald's of Indian food." Maybe he will, in Miami or the Gulf coast. He had a British passport and he could always claim mistreatment at the hands of crazy blacks. His heart wasn't in Toronto. Mohan is right; those who can run, do.

At five minutes after five came the call we always listened for. Two rings, then nothing. We had a drill. The little cook dove under the sink and piled the biggest aluminum platters around him. I locked the door. Gupta looked unconcerned, and he couldn't move anyway. Right then I knew he must have his papers. He just flipped the lamb chops over, then slid the broiler pan back under the flames. Mohan and I headed for the basement and since I was taller, I unscrewed the lightbulb on the way down.

That wasn't the first time. We knew where to hide, Mohan and I. We even had bedrolls on the shelves behind the sacks of rice. We could hear the Mounties up in the kitchen, and we didn't know how Gupta would handle himself. Sometimes they'll let one of us off, if he can turn in three or four.

I knew it was all over when they opened the door to

the basement. "Light?" one of them called out. They sounded like they were right on top of us. One carried a torch, brighter than a searchlight.

"What have we here, eh?" He was a big fellow, blond with a rusty-colored mustache, and he knew exactly where to look. The other was in plain clothes, an immigration officer. They travelled in twos, acting on tips.

They took us up to the kitchen. "There's another one," said the immigration man. Aziz-*sahib* has enemies, and jealous friends. Someone else bought a little time for himself. We are all pawns.

"You, too," said the Mountie, pointing to Gupta. "We're all going down to the station."

"This is a business establishment," said Gupta. "I am responsible here while the owner is away."

"We're closing you down. When the owner comes back we'll get him too."

Mohan was crying. For all his Bombay smart-talk, I could see he was very young, maybe only twenty. Gupta the chef was propped up in his strange way against the sink and the small cabinet underneath it where the assistant cook was hiding. I had a silly thought just then: if they find him, what will he do with his hundred-and-fifty-dollar boots?

"Get out of my kitchen," said Gupta. "Get out immediately."

"It's cold. Get your coats," said the Mountie. "That goes for you, too." It had become a personal thing between them.

"He is a lame man, sir," I said, "He cannot move without his crutches."

"I don't care if I have to sling him over my shoulder—he's coming with us now."

The plainclothesman stepped between them. "It will only go harder if you resist," he said.

"I am not resisting. I am ordering you away from here." His voice was very quiet, but I could see the color rising in his neck.

"Very well," said the Mountie, and he was suddenly in motion, two quick steps toward the chef, one arm out to grab his neck, the other to club him if necessary. But the chef was quicker. All he had to do was slide his hand along the rim of the sink. The Mountie saw it the same time I did—the cleaver—but he didn't have time to react. Gupta whirled, falling as he took a step, with the cleaver high over his head. He brought it down in a wild, practiced chop on the Mountie's outstretched arm, and I could tell from the way it stuck, the way Gupta couldn't extract it easily for a second swing, that it had sunk well below the overcoat and service jacket. The Mountie and Gupta fell simultaneously, and now Gupta was reaching into his back pocket while the screaming Mountie rolled on one side.

Gupta managed to sit straight. He held his Canadian passport in front of his face. That way, he never saw the drawn gun, nor did he try to dodge the single bullet.

Hindus

I RAN into Pat at Sotheby's on a Friday morning two years ago. Derek and I had gone to view the Fraser Collection of Islamic miniatures at the York Avenue galleries. It bothered Derek that I knew so little about my heritage. Islam is nothing more than a marauder's faith to me, but the Mogul emperors stayed a long time in the green delta of the Ganges, flattening and reflattening a fort in the village where I was born, and forcing my priestly ancestors to prove themselves brave. Evidence on that score is still inconclusive. That village is now in Bangladesh.

Derek was a filmmaker, lightly employed at that time. We had been married three hundred and thirty-one days.

"So," Pat said, in his flashy, plummy, drawn-out intonation, "you finally made it to the States!"

It was one of those early November mornings when the woodsy smell of overheated bodies in cloth coats clogged the public stairwells. Everywhere around me I detected the plaintive signs of over-preparedness.

"Whatever are you doing here?" He engulfed me in

a swirl of Liberty scarf and cashmere lapels.

"Trying to get the woman there to sell me the right catalog," I said.

The woman, a very young thing with slippery skin, ate a lusty Granny Smith apple and ignored the dark, hesitant miniature-lovers hanging about like bats in daytime.

"They have more class in London," Pat said.

"I wouldn't know. I haven't been back since that unfortunate year at Roedean."

"It was always New York you wanted," Pat laughed. "Don't say I didn't warn you. The world is full of empty promises."

I didn't remember his having warned me about life and the inevitability of grief. It was entirely possible that he had—he had always been given to clowning pronouncements—but I had not seen him in nine years and in Calcutta he had never really broken through the fortifications of my shyness.

"Come have a drink with me," Pat said.

It was my turn to laugh. "You must meet Derek," I said.

Derek had learned a great deal about India. He could reel off statistics of Panchayati Raj and the electrification of villages and the introduction of mass media, though he reserved his love for birds migrating through the wintry deserts of Jaisalmer. Knowledge of India made Derek more sympathetic than bitter, a common trait of decent outsiders. He was charmed by Pat's heedless, old-world insularity.

"Is this the lucky man?" he said to Derek. He did not hold out his hand. He waved us outside; a taxi magically appeared. "Come have a drink with me tomorrow. At my place."

He gave Derek his card. It was big and would not fit into a wallet made to hold Visa and American Express. Derek read it with his usual curiosity.

H.R.H. Maharajah Patwant Singh
of
Gotlah
Purveyor and Exporter

He tucked the card in the pocket of his raincoat. "I'll be shooting in Toronto tomorrow," he said, "but I'm sure Leela would like to keep it."

There was, in the retention of those final "h's"— even Indian maps and newspapers now referred to Gotla and to maharajas, and I had dropped the old "Leelah" in my first month in America—something of the reclusive mountebank. "I'm going to the Patels' for dinner tomorrow," I said, afraid that Pat would misread the signs of healthy unpossessiveness in our marriage.

"Come for a drink before. What's the matter, Leela? Turning a prude in your old age?" To Derek he explained, "I used to rock her on my knee when she was four. she was gorgeous then, but I am no lecher."

It is true that I was very pretty at four and that Pat spent a lot of time in our house fondling us children. He brought us imported chocolates in beautiful tins and made a show of giving me the biggest. In my family, in every generation, one infant seems destined to be the repository of the family's comeliness. In my generation, I inherited the looks, like an heirloom, to keep in good condition and pass on to the next. Beauty teaches hu-

mility and responsibility in the culture I came from. By
marrying well, I could have seen to the education of
my poorer cousins.

Pat was in a third floor sublet in Gramercy Park South.
A West Indian doorman with pendulous cheeks and an
unbuttoned jacket let me into the building. He didn't
give me a chance to say where I was going as I moved
toward the elevator.

"The Maharaja is third floor, to the right. All the
way down."

I had misunderstood the invitation. It was not to be
an hour of wit and nostalgia among exotic knick-knacks
squirreled into New York from the Gotla Palace. I
counted thirty guests in the first quarter hour of my
short stay. Plump young men in tight-fitting suits scut-
tled from living room to kitchen, balancing overfull
glasses of gin and tonic. The women were mostly
blondes, with luridly mascaraed, brooding eyes, blonde
the way South Americans are blonde, with deep resid-
ual shading. I tried to edge into a group of three women.
One of them said, "I thought India was spellbinding.
Naresh's partner managed to get us into the Lake Palace
Hotel."

"I don't think I could take the poverty," said her
friend, as I retreated.

The living room walls were hung with prints of British East India Company officials at work and play, the
vestibule with mirror-images of Hindu gods and goddesses.

"Take my advice," a Gujarati man said to Pat in the
dim and plantless kitchen. "Get out of diamonds—

emeralds *won't* bottom out. These days it *has* to be rubies and emeralds.''

In my six years in Manhattan I had not entered a kitchen without plants. There was not even a straggly avocado pushing its nervous way out of a shrivelling seed.

I moved back into the living room where the smell of stale turmeric hung like yellow fog from the ceiling. A man rose from the brocade-covered cushions of a banquette near me and plumped them, smiling, to make room for me.

''You're Pat's niece, no?'' the man was francophone, a Lebanese. ''Pat has such pretty nieces. You have just come from Bombay? I love Bombay. Personally, Bombay to me is like a jewel. Like Paris, like Beirut before, now like Bombay. You agree?''

I disclaimed all kinship to H.R.H. I was a Bengali Brahmin; maharajas—not to put too sharp a point on it—were frankly beneath me, by at least one caste, though some of them, like Pat, would dispute it. Before my marriage to Derek no one in my family since our initial eruption from Vishnu's knee had broken caste etiquette. I disclaimed any recent connection with India. ''I haven't been home in ages,'' I told the Lebanese. ''I am an American citizen.''

''I too am. I am American,'' he practically squealed. He rinsed his glass with a bit of gin still left in the bottom, as though he were trying to dislodge lemon pulp stuck and drying on its sides. ''You want to have dinner with me tonight, yes? I know Lebanese places, secret and intimate. Food and ambiance very romantic.''

''She's going to the Patels'.'' It was Pat. The Gujarati

with advice on emeralds was still lodged in the kitchen, huddling with a stocky blonde in a fuchsia silk sari.

"Oh, the Patels," said the Lebanese. "You did not say. Super guy, no? He's doing all right for himself. Not as well as me, of course. I own ten stores and he only has four."

Why, I often asked myself, was Derek never around to share these intimacies? Derek would have drawn out the suave, French-speaking, soulful side of this Seventh Avenue *shmattiste*.

It shouldn't have surprised me that the Lebanese man in the ruffled shirt should have known Mohan and Motibehn Patel. For immigrants in similar trades, Manhattan is still a village. Mohan had been in the States for eighteen years and last year had become a citizen. They'd been fortunate in having only sons, now at Cal Tech and Cornell; with daughters there would have been pressure on them to return to India for a proper, arranged marriage.

"Is he still in Queens?"

"No," I told him. "They've moved to a biggish old place on Central Park West."

"Very foolish move," said the Lebanese. "They will only spend their money now." He seemed genuinely appalled.

Pat looked at me surprised. "I can't believe it," he exclaimed. "Leela Lahiri actually going crosstown at night by herself. I remember when your Daddy wouldn't let you walk the two blocks from school to the house without that armed Nepali, what was his name, dogging your steps."

"Gulseng," I said. "He was run over by a lorry three

years ago. I think his name was really something-or-other-Rana, but he never corrected us.''

''Short, nasty and brutal,'' said Pat. ''They don't come that polite and loyal these days. Just as likely to slit your throat as anyone else, these days.''

The Lebanese, sensing the end of brave New World overtures, the gathering of the darknesses we shared, drifted away.

''The country's changed totally, you know,'' Pat continued. ''Crude rustic types have taken over. The *dhoti-wallahs*, you know what I mean, they would wrap themselves in loincloths if it got them more votes. No integrity, no finesse. The country's gone to the dogs, I tell you.''

''That whole life's outmoded, Pat. Obsolete. All over the world.''

''They tried to put me in jail,'' he said. His face was small with bitterness and alarm. ''They didn't like my politics, I tell you. Those Communists back home arrested me and threw me in jail. Me. Like a common criminal.''

''On what charges?''

''Smuggling. For selling family heirlooms to Americans who understand them. No one at home understands their value. Here, I can sell off a little Pahari painting for ten thousand dollars. Americans understand our things better than we do ourselves. India wants me to starve in my overgrown palace.''

''Did you really spend a night in jail?'' I couldn't believe that modernization had finally come to India and that even there, no one was immune from consequences.

''Three nights!'' he fumed. ''Like a common *dacoit*.

The country has no respect anymore. The country has nothing. It has driven us abroad with whatever assets we could salvage.''

"You did well, I take it." I did not share his perspective; I did not feel my country owed me anything. Comfort, perhaps, when I was there; a different comfort when I left it. India teaches her children: you have seen the worst. Now go out and don't be afraid.

"I have nothing," he spat. "They've stripped me of everything. At night I hear the jackals singing in the courtyard of my palace.''

But he had recovered by the time I left for the cross-town cab ride to the Patels. I saw him sitting on the banquette where not too long before the Lebanese had invited me to share an evening of unwholesomeness. On his knee he balanced, a tall, silver-haired woman who looked like Candice Bergen. She wore a pink cashmere sweater which she must have put through the washing machine. Creases, like worms, curled around her sweatered bosom.

I didn't see Pat for another two years. In those two years I did see a man who claimed to have bounced the real Candice Bergen on his knee. He had been a juggler at one time, had worked with Edgar Bergen on some vaudeville act and could still pull off card tricks and walk on his hands up and down my dining table. I kept the dining table when Derek and I split last May. He went back to Canada which we both realized too late he should never have left and the table was too massive to move out of our West 11th Street place and into his downtown Toronto, chic renovated apartment. The ex-juggler is my boss at a publishing house. My job is

menial but I have a soothing title. I am called an Ad-
ministrative Assistant.

In the two years I have tried to treat the city not as
an island of dark immigrants but as a vast sea in which
new Americans like myself could disappear and resur-
face at will. I did not avoid Indians, but without Derek's
urging for me to be proud of my heritage, I did not
seek them out. The Patels did invite me to large dinners
where all the guests seemed to know with the first flick
of their eyes in my direction that I had married a white
man and was now separated, and there our friendships
hit rock. I was a curiosity, a novel and daring element
in the community; everyone knew my name. After a
while I began to say I was busy to Motibehn Patel.

Pat came to the office with my boss, Bill Haines, the
other day. "I wanted you to meet one of our new au-
thors, Leela," Bill said.

"Leela, *dar-ling*!" Pat cried. His voice was shrill
with enthusiasm, and he pressed me histrionically
against his Burberry raincoat. I could feel a button tap
my collarbone. "It's been years! Where have you been
hiding your gorgeous self?"

"I didn't realize you two knew each other," Bill said.

All Indians in America, I could have told him, con-
stitute a village.

"Her father bailed me out when the Indian government sought to persecute me," he said with a pout. "If
it hadn't been for courageous friends like her daddy, I
and my poor subjects might just as well have kicked
the bucket."

"She's told me nothing about India," said Bill
Haines. "No accent, Western clothes—"

"Yes, a shame, that. By the way, Leela, I just found a picture of Lahiri-*sahab* on an elephant when I was going through my official papers for Bill. If you come over for drinks—after getting out of those ridiculous clothes, I must insist—I can give it to you. Lahiri-*sahab* looks like Ernest Hemingway in that photo. You tell him I said he looks like Hemingway."

"Daddy's in Ranikhet this month," I said. "He's been bedridden for a while. Arthritis. He's just beginning to move around a bit again."

"I have hundreds of good anecdotes, Bill, about her Daddy and me doing *shikar* in the Sundarban forest. Absolutely *huge* Bengal tigers. I want to balance the politics—which as you rightly say are central—with some stirring bits about what it was like in the good old days."

"What are you writing?" I asked.

"I thought you'd never ask, my dear. My memoirs. At night I leave a Sony by my bed. Night is the best time for remembering. I hear the old sounds and voices. You remember, Leela, how the palace ballroom used to hum with dancing feet on my birthdays?"

"Memoirs of a Modern Maharajah," Bill Haines said.

"I seem to remember the singing of jackals," I said, not unkindly, though he chose to ignore it.

"Writing is what keeps me from going through death's gate. There are nights . . ." He didn't finish. His posture had stiffened with self-regard; he communicated great oceans of anguish. He'd probably do well. It was what people wanted to hear.

"The indignities," he said suddenly. "The atrocities." He stared straight ahead, at a watercooler. "The nights in jail, the hyenas sniffing outside your barred window. I will never forget their smell, never! It is the smell of death, Leela. The new powers-that-be are peasants. Peasants! They cannot know, they cannot suspect how they have made me suffer. The country is in the hands of tyrannical peasants!''

"Look, Pat," Bill Haines said, leading the writer toward his office, "I have to see Bob Savage, the subrights man one floor down. Make yourself at home. Just pull down any book you want to read. I'll be back in a minute."

"Don't worry about me. I shall be all right, Bill. I have my Sony in my pocket. I shall just sit in a corner beside the daughter of my oldest friend, this child I used to bounce on my knee, and I shall let my mind skip into the nooks and crannies of Gotlah Palace. Did I tell you, when I was a young lad my mother kept pet crocs? Big, huge gents and ladies with ugly jaws full of nasty teeth. They were her pets. She gave them names and fed them chickens every day. Come to me, Padma. Come to me, Prem."

"It'll be dynamite," Bill Haines said. "The whole project's dynamite." He pressed my hand as he eased his stubby, muscular body past the stack of dossiers on my desk. "And *you'll* be a godsend in developing this project."

"And what's with you?" Pat asked me. I could tell he already knew the essentials.

"Nothing much." But he wasn't listening anyway.

"You remember the thief my security men caught in the early days of your father's setting up a factory in my hills? You remember how the mob got excited and poured acid on his face?"

I remembered. Was the Sony recording it? Was the memory an illustration of swift and righteous justice in a collapsed Himalayan princely state, or was it the savage and disproportionate fury of a people resisting change?

"Yes, certainly I do. Can I get you a cup of coffee? Or tea?" That, of course, was an important part of my job.

"No thanks," he said with a flutter of his wrinkled hands. "I have given up all stimulants. I've even given up bed-tea. It interferes with my writing. Writing is everything to me nowadays. It has been my nirvana."

"The book sounds dynamite," I assured him. An Indian woman is brought up to please. No matter how passionately we link bodies with our new countries, we never escape the early days.

Pat dropped his voice, and, stooping conspiratorially, said to me in Hindi, "There's one big favor you can do for me, though. Bill has spoken of a chap I should be knowing. Who is this Edgar Bergen?"

"I think he was the father of a movie actress," I said. I, too, had gone through the same contortion of recognition with Bill Haines. Fortunately, like most Americans, he could not conceive of a world in which Edgar Bergen had no currency. Again in Hindi, Pat asked me for directions to the facilities, and this time I could give a full response. He left his rolled-slim umbrella propped against my desk and walked toward the fountain.

"Is he really a maharaja?" Lisa leaned over from her desk to ask me. She is from Rhode Island. Brown hasn't cured her of responding too enthusiastically to each call or visit from a literary personage. "He's terrific. So suave and distinguished! Have you known him from way back when?''

"Yes," I said, all the way from when.

"I had no idea you spoke Hindu. It's eerie to think you can speak such a hard language. I'm having trouble enough with French. I keep forgetting that you haven't lived here always.''

I keep forgetting it too. I was about to correct her silly mistake—I'd learned from Derek to be easily incensed over ignorant confusions between Hindi and Hindu—but then I thought, why bother? Maybe she's right. That slight undetectable error, call it an accent, isn't part of language at all. I speak Hindu. No matter what language I speak it will come out slightly foreign, no matter how perfectly I mouth it. There's a whole world of us now, speaking Hindu. The manuscript of *Memoirs* was not dynamite, but I stayed up all night to finish it. In spite of the arch locutions and the aggrieved posture that Pat had stubbornly clung to, I knew I was reading about myself, blind and groping conquistador who had come to the New World too late.

Saints

"AND one more thing," Mom says. "Your father can't take you this August."

I can tell from the way she fusses with the placemats that she is interested in my reaction. The placemats are made of pinkish linen and I can see a couple of ironing marks, like shiny little arches. Wayne is coming for dinner. Wayne Latta is her new friend. It's the first time she's having him over with others, but that's not why she's nervous.

"That's okay," I tell her. "Tran and I have plans for the summer."

Mom rolls up the spray-starched napkins and knots them until they look like nesting birds on each dinner plate. "It isn't that he's really busy," she says. She gives me one of her I-know-you're-hurting, son, looks. "I don't see why he can't take you. He says he has a conference to go to in Hong Kong at the end of July, so he might as well do China in August."

"It's okay. Really," I say. It's true, I am okay. At fifteen I'm too old to be a pawn between them, and too

122

young to get caught in problems of my own. I'm in a state of grace. I want to get to my room in this state of grace before it disintegrates, and start a new game of "Geopolitique 1990" on the Apple II-Plus Dad gave me last Christmas.

"Can you get the flower holders, Shawn?" Mom asks.

I take a wide, flat cardboard box out of the buffet.

She lifts eight tiny glass holders out of the box, and lines them up in the center of the table. She hasn't used them since things started going bad between Dad and her. When things blew up, they sold the big house in New Jersey and Mom and I moved to this college town in upstate New York. Mom works in the Admissions Office. Wayne calls it a college for rich bitches who were too dumb to get into Bennington or Barnard.

"Get me a pitcher of water and the flowers," Mom says.

In a dented aluminum pot in the kitchen sink, eight yellow rosebuds are soaking up water. Granules of sugar are whitish and still sludgy in the bottom of the pot. Mom's a believer; she's read somewhere that sugar in lukewarm water keeps cut flowers fresh. I move the pot to one side and fill a quart-sized measuring cup with lukewarm water. I know her routines.

It's going to be an anxious evening for Mom. She's set out extra goblets for spritzers on a tray lined with paper towels. Index cards typed up with recipes for dips and sauces are stacked on the windowsill. She shouldn't do sauces, nothing that requires last-minute frying and stirring. She's the flustery type, and she's only setting herself up for failure.

"What happened to the water, Shawn?"

It's a Pizza Hut night for me, definitely. I know what she's going through with Wayne. He's not at all like Dad, the good Dr. Manny Patel, who soothes crazies at Creedmore all day. Nights he's a playboy and slum landlord, Mom says.

Mom says, "Your father will call you tomorrow, he said. He wants to talk to you himself. He wants to know what you want this Christmas."

This is only the first Thursday in November. Dad's planning ahead is a joke with us. Foresight is what got him out of Delhi to New York. "Could I have become a psychiatrist and a near-millionaire if I hadn't planned well ahead?" Dad used to tell Mom in the medium-bad days.

Mom thinks making a million is a vicious, selfish aim. But Dad's really very generous. He sends money to relatives and to Indian orphanages. He's generous but practical. He says he doesn't want to send me stuff— cashmere sweaters and Ultrasuede jackets, the stuff he likes—that'll end up in basement cedar closets.

"I'll be late tomorrow," I remind Mom. "Fridays I have my chess club."

Actually, Tran and I and a bunch of other guys from the chess club play four afternoons a week. Thursdays we don't play because Tran has Debate Workshop.

"You know what I want, Mom. You can tell him."

I ask for computer games, video cassettes, nothing major. So twice a year Dad sends big checks. Dad's real generous with me. It makes him feel the big bene-factor, Mom says, whenever a check comes in the mail. But that's only because things went really bad two years ago. They sent me away to boarding school, but they still couldn't work things out between them.

At five, Wayne comes into our driveway in his blue Toyota pickup. The wheels squeal and rock in the deep, snowy ruts. Wayne has a cord of firewood in the back of the truck. Mom paid him for the firewood yesterday and for the time he put in picking up the cord from some French guy in Ballston Spa. Wayne's a writer; meantime he works as a janitor in the college. A "mop-ologist" is what he calls himself. It's so corny, but every time Wayne uses that word, Mom gives him a tinkly, supportive laugh. Janitors are more caring than shrinks, the laugh seems to say.

We hear Wayne on the back porch, cursing as he drops an armload of logs. For all his muscles, he's a clumsy man. But then Mom could never have gotten Dad to carry the logs himself. Dad would have had them delivered or done without them.

Mom takes five-dollar bills out of the buffet drawer and counts out thirty dollars. "For the wine, would you give it to him? I couldn't do a production all by myself on a weeknight."

"Why do a production at all?"

She stiffens. "I'm not ashamed of Wayne," she says. "Wayne is who he is."

Wayne finally comes into the dining room. I slip him the money; it's more than he expected. "I got some beer too, Mila." Mom's name is Camille but he calls her Mila. That's a hard thing to get used to. He drops my rucksack on the floor, turns the chair around and straddles it. There are five other chairs around the table and two folding chairs brought up from the basement for tonight. Under Wayne's muscular thighs, the dining room chair looks rickety, absurdly elegant. Red long-johns show through the knee rips of his blue jeans.

He keeps his red knit cap on. But he's not as tough as he looks. He keeps the cap on because he's sensitive about his bald, baby-pink head.

"Hey, Shawn," he says to me. "Still baking the competition?"

It's Wayne's usual joke about my playing competitive chess. Our school team has T-shirts that we paid for by working the concession stands on basketball nights last winter. Tran plays varsity first board, I play third. Now we need chess cheerleaders, Wayne kids me. *"Hey, hey, push that pawn! Dee-fense, dee-fense, King's Indian dee-fense!"* Wayne isn't a bad sort, not for around here. Last year we went for trout out on the Battenkill. The day with Wayne wasn't bad, given our complicated situation. I went back to the creek with Tran a week later, but it was different. Tran's idea of fishing is throwing a net across the river, tossing in a stick of dynamite, then pulling it up.

"You'll like Milos and Verna," Mom tells Wayne. "They're both painters in the Art Department. From Yugoslavia, but I think they're hoping to stay in the States."

From the soft, nervous look she's giving Wayne, I know it isn't the Yugoslavs she's thinking of right at the moment. Wayne grabs her throat in his thick hairy hands. She lifts her face. Then she glances at me in a quick guilty way as if she's already given away too much.

I know about feelings. I've got a secret life, too.

"D'you have enough for a pizza?" Mom asks me. She's moved away from Wayne.

Yeah, I have enough.

* * *

From the Pizza Hut, Tran and I go back to Tran's place. Tran's sixteen and he owns a noisy used Plymouth. It's two-tone, white and aquamarine. I like the colors. Tran's a genuine boatperson. When he was younger, the English teacher made him tell the class about having to hide from pirates and having to chew on raw fish just to stay alive. Women on his boat hid any valuable stuff they had in their vaginas. "That's enough, Tran, thank you," the teacher said. Now he never mentions his cruise to America.

We skid to a stop inside the Indian Lookout Point Trailer Park where he lives with his mother in a flash of aqua. The lights are on in Tran's mobile home. Tran's mother's muddy Chevy and his stepfather's Dodge Ram are angle-parked. Tran's real father got left behind in Saigon.

"I don't know," Tran says. He doesn't cut the engine. We sit in the warm, dark car. "Maybe we ought to go on to your place. He never gets home this early."

It's minus ten outside, maybe worse with the windchill factor. I open the car door softly. The carlight on Tran's face makes his face look ochre-dingy, mottled with pimples.

"Mom's entertaining tonight," I warn him. The snow is slippery cold under my Adidas. I pick my way through icy patches to the trailer, and look in a little front window.

Tran's mom is at the kitchen sink, washing a glass. She's still wearing her wool coat and plaid scarf. Her face has an odd puffy quiver. There are no signs of physical violence, but someone's sure been hurt. Tran's stepfather (he didn't, and can't, adopt Tran until some agency can locate Tran's real father, and get his consent) is sitting hunched forward in a rocker, and drinking Miller Lite.

Like Tran, I've learned to discount homey scenes.

"That's okay," Tran says. He's calling out from the car. His sad face is in the opened window. "Your place is bigger."

It makes sense, but I can't move away from his little window.

"I can show you a move that'll bake Sato," he says. "I mean really bake his ass."

We both hate Sato but Sato isn't smart enough to wince under our hate or even smart enough to know when his ass has really been baked.

"Okay." There's that new killer chess move, and a new Peter Gabriel for us to listen to. Tran's chess rating is just under 1900. Farelli's is higher, but Farelli is more than arrogant. He's so arrogant he dropped off the team. He goes down to Manhattan instead and hustles games in Times Square or in the chess clubs. Tran's a little guilty about playing first board; he knows he owes it to Farelli's vanity. The difference between Farelli and Tran is about the same as between Tran and me. Farelli wants to charge the club four-fifty an hour for tutoring. He's the only real American in the club. The rest of us have names like Sato, Chin, Duoc, Cho and Prasad. My name's Patel, Shawn Patel. Mom took back her maiden name, Belliveau, when we moved out of Upper Montclair. We're supposed to be out of Dad's reach here, except for checks.

A week after Mom's dinner party, Tran and I are coming out of an arcade on Upper Broadway Street when we see Wayne walking our way. Upper Broadway's short and squat. The storefronts have shallow doorways you can't hide in. Wayne is with the Yugoslav woman, the painter who doesn't intend to go back to her country. They aren't holding hands or anything, they aren't even touching shoulders, but I can tell they want to do things. The Yugoslav has both her hands in the pockets of her duffle coat. A toggle at her throat is missing and the loop has nothing to weigh it down. The Yugoslav has red cheeks. With her red cheeks, her button nose and her long, loose hair, she looks very young. Maybe it's a trick of afternoon light or of European make-up, but she looks too young to be a friend of Mom's.

Wayne wants to hug her. I can tell from the way he arches his upper body inside his coat. He wants to sneak his hand into her pocket, pull out her fist, swing hands on Upper Broadway and be stared at by everyone.

I pull Tran back inside the arcade.

"I got to get to Houston," Tran says. We're playing "Joust," his favorite game, but his slight body is twisted in misery.

"It'll work out," I tell him. Wanting to go to Houston has to do with his mother and stepfather. Things always go bad between parents. "You can't leave in the middle of the semester. It doesn't make sense."

"What does?"

Tran has an older brother in Houston, in engineering school. Tran thinks his mother will come up with the bus fare south. She works at Grand Union, and weekends she waitresses. "My luck's got to change," he says.

Luck has nothing to do with anything, I want to say. You're out of the clutch of pirates now. No safe hiding places.

Wayne and his painter make us spend too many tokens on this Joust machine.

Mom's in the eating nook of the kitchen, reading a book
on English gardens when I come in the back door. She's
wearing a long skirt made of quilted fabric and a matching jacket. The quilting makes her look fat, and ridiculous.

She catches my grin. "It's warm, don't knock it,"
she says of her skirt. These upstate houses are drafty.
Then she pulls her feet up under her and wriggles her
raised knees gracelessly under the long skirt. "And I
love the color on me."

I bleed. Mom should have had a daughter. Two
women could have consoled each other. I can only think
of Wayne, how even now he's slipping the loops over
Serbian toggles. It's a complicated feeling. I bleed because I'm disloyal.

"Your father's sent a present by UPS," she says. She
doesn't look up from the illustration of a formal garden
of a lord. A garden with a stiff, bristly hedged maze to
excite desire and contain it. "I put the package on your
desk upstairs. It looks like a book."

She means to say, Dad's present are always impersonal.

Actually it's two books that Dad has sent me this
time. The thick, heavy one is an art book, reproductions of Moghul paintings that Dad loves. Even India
was once an empire-building nation. The other is a thin
book with bad binding put out by a religious printing
house in Madras. The little book is about a Hindu saint
who had visions. Dad has sent me a book about visions.

May this book bring you as much happiness as it did

me when I was your age.'' Dad's inscription reads. Then a p.s. ''The saint died of throat cancer and was briefly treated by your great-uncle, the cancer specialist in Calcutta.''

Forty pages into the book, the saint describes a vision. ''I see the Divine Mother in all things.'' He sees Her in ants, dogs, flowers, the latrine bowls in the temple. He keeps falling into trances as he goes for walks or as he says his prayers. In this perfect state, sometimes the saint kicks his disciples. He eats garbage thrown out by temple cooks for cows and pariah dogs.

''Did I kick you?'' the saint asks when he comes out of his trance. ''Kick, kick,'' beg the disciples as they push each other to get near enough for a saintly touch.

My father, healer of derangements, slum landlord with income properties on two continents, believer of visions, pleasure-taker where none seems present, is a mystery.

Downstairs Mom is dialing Wayne's number. In the whir of the telephone dial, I read the new rhythms of her agony. Wayne will not answer his phone tonight. Wayne is in bed with his naked Yugoslav.

It's my turn to call. I slip my bony finger into the dial's fingerholes. ''Want to ball?'' I whisper into the mouthpiece. My throat is raspy from the fullness of desire.

''What?'' It's a girlish voice at the other end. ''What did you say?''

The girl giggles. ''You dumb pervert.'' She leaves it to me to hang up first.

The next night, a Friday night, Tran and I come down from my room to get Mountain Dew out of the fridge.

Mom and Wayne are making out in the kitchen. He has her jammed up against the eating nook's wall. There are Indian paintings on that wall. She kept the paintings and gave Dad the statues and framed batiks. Wayne holds Mom's head against dusty glass, behind which an emperor in Moghul battledress is leading his army out of the capital. Wayne's got his knee high up Mom's quilted skirt. The knee presses in, hard. I see love's monstrous force bloat her face. Wayne has her head in his grasp. Her orange hair tufts out between his knuckles, and its orange mist covers the bygone emperor and his soldiers.

Tran's used to living in small, usurped spaces. He drops a shy, civil little cough, and right away Wayne lets go of Mom's hair. But his knee is still raised, still pressing into her skirt.

"Get outta here, guys," he says. He looks pleased, he sounds good-natured. "You got better things to do. Go push your pawns."

"Tell her about the painter," I say. My voice is even, not emotional.

"What're you talking about? What's the matter with you?"

Tran says, "let's get the soda, Shawn." He picks up the six-pack and two glasses and pushes me toward the stairwell.

Upstairs, Tran and I take turns dialling the town's other insomniacs. "Do you have soft breasts?" I ask. I really want to know. "Yes," one of them confesses. "Very soft and very white and I'm so lonely tonight. Do you want to touch?"

Tran reads aloud an episode from the life of the Hindu saint. Reaching the state of perfection while strolling along the Ganges one day, the saint fell and broke his arm. The saint had been thinking of his love for the young boy followers who lived in the temple. He had been thinking of his love for them—love as for a sweetheart, he says—when he slipped into a trance and stumbled. Love and pain: in the saint's mind there is no separation.

Tran makes the last of our calls for the night. "You bitch," he says as he shakes his thin body in a parody of undulation. To me he says, "Mother won't come through with the bus fare to Houston."

Tonight Tran wants to sleep over in my room. Tomorrow we'll find a way to raise the bus fare.

I want to tell him things, to console him. Bad luck and good luck even out over a lifetime. Cancer can ravage an ecstatic saint. Things pass. I don't remember Dad in any intimate way except that he embarrassed me when he came to pick me up from my old boarding school. The overstated black Mercedes, the hugging and kissing in such a foreign way.

A little before midnight, Tran's moan startles me awake. He must be dreaming of fathers, pirates, saints and Houston. For me the worst isn't dreams. It's having to get out of the house at night and walk around. At midnight I float like a ghost through other people's gardens. I peer into other boys' bedrooms, I become somebody else's son.

Tonight I'm more restless than other nights. I look for an Indian name in the phone book. The directory in our upstate town is thin; it caves against my eager arms. The first name I spot is Batliwalla. Meaning perhaps bottle-walla, a dealer in bottles in the ancestral long-ago. Batliwalla, Jamshed S., M.D.

I dress in the dark for a night of cold roaming. It'll be a night of walking in a state of perfect grace. For disguise, I choose Mom's red cloth coat from the hall cupboard and her large red wool beret into which she has stuck a pheasant feather. She keeps five more feathers, like a bouquet, in a candy jar. The feathers are from Wayne the hunter. Wayne's promised to put a pheasant on our table for Thanksgiving dinner. I can taste its hard, stringy birdflesh and pellets of buckshot.

Like the Hindu saint, I walk my world in boots and a trance. But in this upstate town the only body of water is an icy creek, not the Ganges.

The Batliwallas have no curtains on their back windows. I look into a back bedroom that glows from a bedside lamp. A kid in pajamas is sitting up in bed, a book in his hands. He's a little kid, a junior high kid, or maybe a studious dwarf. The dwarfkid rocks back and forth under his bedclothes. He seems to be learning something, maybe a poem, by heart. He's the conqueror of alien syllables. His fleshy, brown lips purse and pout ferociously. His tiny head in its helmet of glossy black hair bumps, bumps, bumps the bed's white vinyl headboard. The dwarfkid's eyes are screwed tightly shut, and his long eyelashes look like tiny troughs for ghosts to drink out of. Wanting good grades, the dwarfkid studies into the night. He rocks, he shouts, he bumps his head. I can't hear the words, but I want to reach out to a fellow saint.

When I get home, the back porch is dark but the kitchen light is on. I sit on the stack of firewood and look in. I'm not cold, or sleepy. Wayne and Mom are fighting in the kitchen, literally slugging each other. I had Wayne figured wrong. He isn't the sly operator after all. He's opened up my Mom's upper lip. It's blood Mom is washing off.

"Get out," Mom screams at him. This time I can make out all the words. I feel like a god, overseeing lives.

The faucet is running as it had done the day there were yellow rosebuds in a kitchen pot. Steam from the hot, running water frizzes Mom's hair. She looks old. "Get out of my house."

"I'm getting out." Wayne says. But he doesn't leave. First he lights a cigarette, something Mom doesn't permit. Then he flops down on one of the two kitchen stools, props his workboots on the other and starts to adjust the laces. "I wouldn't stay if you begged me."

"Get out, out!" Mom's still screaming as I turn my house key in the lock. She might as well know it all. "Do me a favor, get out. Lace your goddamn boots in your goddamn truck. Please get out."

I move through the bright kitchen into the dark dining room, and wait for the lovers to finish.

In a while Wayne leaves. He doesn't slam the door. He doesn't toss the key on the floor. The pickup's low beams dance on frozen bushes.

"My god, Shawn!" Mom has switched on a wall light in the dining room. She's staring at me, she's really looking at me. Finally. "My god, what have you done to your face, poor baby."

Her fingers scrape at the muck on my face, the cheek-blush, lipstick, eyeshadow. Her bruised mouth is on my hair. I can feel her warm, wet sobs, but I don't hurt. I am in a trance in the middle of a November night. I can't hurt for me, for Dad, I can't hurt for anyone in the world. I feel so strong, so much a potentate in battledress.

How wondrous to be a visionary. If I were to touch someone now, I'd be touching god.

Visitors

WHEN Vinita lived in Calcutta, she had many admirers. Every morning at ten minutes after nine o'clock when she left home for Loreto College where she majored in French literature, young men with surreptitious hands slipped love notes through the half-open windows of her father's car and were sternly rebuked by the chauffeur. The notes were almost always anonymous; when she read them in class, tucked between the pages of Rimbaud and Baudelaire, the ferocity of passion never failed to thrill and alarm her.

For a time after college she worked as a receptionist in the fancy downtown Chowringhee office of a multinational corporation. She had style, she had charm, and everyone genuinely liked her. Especially two junior executives from the fifth floor which was occupied by a company that exported iron manhole covers. If it hadn't been for Vinita's tact, and her ability to make each of the suitors feel that he was the one who made her happier, the two men might have become embittered rivals.

She was quietly convivial and on weekdays went, usually in a group of six or eight, for Chinese lunches to the Calcutta Club. Even the club waiters brightened up when they saw Vinita, though she had never actually been heard to say anything more personal to them than, "A lime soda, please, no ice," or "I'll have the Chou En Lai carp."

She had known all along that after marriage she would have to leave Calcutta. Her parents wanted to marry her off to a doctor or engineer of the right caste and class but resident abroad, preferably in America. The groom they finally selected for her was a thirty-five-year-old accountant, Sailen Kumar, a well-mannered and amiable-looking man, a St. Stephen's graduate who had gone on to London University and Harvard and who now worked for a respectable investment house in Manhattan and lived in a two-bedroom condominium with access to gym, pool and sauna across the river. He was successful—and well off, Vinita's parents decided—by anyone's standards. Six days after the wedding, Vinita took an Air India flight to citizenship in the New World.

Marriage suits Vinita. In the months she has been a wife in Guttenberg, New Jersey, she has become even prettier. Her long black hair has a gloss that owes as much to a new sense of well-being as to the new shampoos she tries out and that leave her head smelling of herbs, fruits and flowers. Her surroundings—the sleek Bloomingdale's furniture Sailen had bought just before flying out to find a bride in India, the coordinated linen for bed and bath, and the wide, gleaming appliances in the kitchenette—please her. She finds it hard to believe that she has been gifted the life of grace and ease that

she and her Loreto College friends had coveted from
reading old copies of *Better Homes and Gardens* in Calcutta. This life of grace and ease has less to do with
modern conveniences such as the microwave oven built
into a narrow wall which is covered with designer wallpaper, and more to do with moods and traits she rec-
ognizes as new in herself. Happiness, expressiveness,
bad temper: all these states seem valuable and exciting
to her. But she is not sure she deserves this life. She
has done nothing exceptional. She has made no brave
choices. The decision to start over on a new continent
where hard work is more often than not rewarded with
comfort has been her parents', not hers. If her father
had brought her a proposal and photograph from an
upright hydraulics engineer living in a government project site in the wilds of Durgapur or from a rich radi-
ologist with a clinic on a quiet boulevard in South
Calcutta, she would have accepted the proposal with the
same cheerfulness she has shown Sailen Kumar. She's
a little taken aback by the idea of just desserts. Back
home good fortune had been exactly that: a matter of
luck and fortune, a deity's decision to humor and in-
dulge. She remembered the fables she read as a child
in which a silly peasant might find a pitcher of gold
mohurs on his way to the village tank for his bath. But
in America, at least in New Jersey, everyone Vinita
meets seems to acknowledge a connection between
merit and reward. Everyone looks busy, distraught from
overwork. Even the building's doorman; she worries
about Castro, the doorman. Such faith in causality can
only lead to betrayal.

Vinita expected married life, especially married life
in a new country and with no relatives around, to change

her. Overnight she would become mature, complex, fascinating: a wife, instead of a daughter. Thoughts of change did not frighten her. Discreet, dutiful, comfortable with her upper-class status, she had been trained by her mother to stay flexible, to roll with whatever punches the Communist government of Calcutta might delive. In Virita's childhood, the city had convulsed through at least two small revolutions. Some nights in Guttenberg, New Jersey, even with her eyes closed, she can see a fresh, male corpse in a monsoon muddy gutter. Her parents still talk of the two boys who had invaded their lawn one heady afternoon of class struggle and pointed pipe-guns at the trembling gardener. Sometimes the designer wallpaper seems to ripple like leaves in a breeze, and she feels herself being watched.

But it's not the corpse, not the undernourished child-rebels, who feed her nightmares. It's nothing specific. She considers fear of newness a self-indulgence, quite unworthy of someone who has wanted all along to exchange her native world for an alien one. The slightest possibility of disruption pleases her. But if change has come into her life as Mrs. Sailen Kumar, it has seeped in so gradually that she can't fix it with one admiring stare when she Windexes toothpaste flecks off the bathroom mirror.

This afternoon Vinita has three visitors. Two of them are women, Mrs. Leela Mehra and Mrs. Kamila Thapar, wives of civil engineers. They stay just long enough to have spiced tea with onion pakoras and to advise her on which Indian grocers carry the freshest tropical pro-
in the "Little India" block on Lexington. Vinita
nvinced the real reason they have come to visit is

to check out what changes she, the bride, has made to Sailen's condominium. They have known her husband for almost ten years. Mr. Thapar and Sailen roomed together when both were new to America (she has trouble visualizing the dark-suited, discreetly groomed men as callow foreign students forty pounds lighter with little money and too much ambition). Sailen, while sketching in his bachelor life—all those years when she had not known that the man of her dreams would have only nine fingers!—had told her how the Thapars and the Mehras made themselves his substitute family in the new world, how they fed him curries most weekends, made him sleep on their lumpy front room sofas instead of letting him take a late-night bus back to Manhattan, and how the two women hummed bits of old Hindi film songs to tease him into nostalgia. Otherwise, they said, he'd become bad-tempered and self-centered, too American. In Mrs. Mehra's and Mrs. Thapar's presence, Vinita is the intruder.

After they leave, Vinita takes out a rubber-banded roll of aerogrammes from a desk built into the wall system. She makes a list of the people she must write today:

1. her parents (a short but vivacious note)
2. her closest Loreto College friend who now works for Air India
3. her married sister in Bombay (it can wait till the weekend)
4. Mother Stella, the Mauritian nun who'd taught her French.

Writing letters on the pale blue aerogramme paper makes her feel cheerful and just a little noble. Writing to Mother Stella puts her in a special mood, a world tinged slightly with poetic, even rhapsodic passion. Even lines of Rimbaud's deemed unsuitable for maidenly Calcutta teenagers were somehow tamed by Mother Stella's exquisite elocution. How preposterous was a passion—*le dos de ces Mains est la place qu'en baisa tout Révolté fier!*—parsed by a half-Indian, French-speaking, Mauritian nun.

She writes her mother, converting each small episode—buying half a dozen cheese Danishes, spraying herself with expensive fragrances from tester atomizers—into grand adventures. When she licks and seals each envelope, she is grateful Sailen agreed to her father's proposal of marriage and that she is now cut off from her moorings. Her letters are intended to please and comfort. She knows that when the postman rings his bicycle bell and keels into the driveway twice a day, the servants, her mother, her sister, her friend and even the nun who has taught her all she knows about literature and good manners run to the front door hoping for a new installment of her idylls in America. But before Vinita can decide what vivacious cliches to end her last letter with, a third visitor arrives at the door and holds out a bright, amateurish poster announcing an Odissi dance recital on the Columbia campus.

"Mrs. Kumar, I thought you would be interested in dance performances," the visitor says. He smiles, but does not step into the tiny hall which is crowded with a pair of Vishnupuri clay horses and a tall, cylindrical Chinese vase that holds umbrellas. "I was afraid that you and Mr. Kumar might not have heard about Rooma Devi coming to Columbia."

"Odissi style?" She knows it is up to her to invite him in or send him away. She has met him, yes, she has talked to him at three, maybe four, cultural evenings organized by one of the Indian Associations in Manhattan. He is a graduate student in history at Columbia.

"Mrs. Kumar, if you don't mind my saying so, the first time I saw you I could tell that you yourself were a dancer. Right?"

She glances at him shyly, and steps back, her slippers grazing the rough clay foot of one of the giant horses. Still she doesn't ask him in. Let him make that decision. In India, she would feel uncomfortable—she knows she would!—if she found herself in an apartment alone with a man not related to her, but the rules are different in Guttenberg. Here one has to size up the situation and make up one's own rules. Or is it, here, that one has to seize the situation?

"You have the grace of a *danseuse*," he says.

Vinita has not heard anyone use the word *danseuse*. She likes the word; it makes her feel elegant and lissom. "I'll have to confess I am. I've danced a bit. But not in years."

She blushes, hoping to pass off for modesty the guilt she feels at having lied. She is not a dancer, not a real dancer. She has studied Rabindra-style dancing for about six years. Her mother, who regarded dancing as necessary a feminine accomplishment as singing and gourmet cooking, had forced the two sisters to take weekly lessons at a fine arts academy in Ballygunge. She looks down at the floor, at his two-tone New Balance running shoes. The shoes deepen her blush. She is in a new country with no rules. No grown man in

India she knows wears gym shoes except for cricket or squash. But there's mud on his New Balances, a half-moon of mud around each toe part. He has taken the bus to Guttenberg, New Jersey, just to make sure that she'll know about the recital. Because he has guessed—he had divined—that she is a *danseuse*.

She takes two hesitant steps back, her left hand entwined with the elongated clay neck of the larger horse. Here, as in India, friends stop by without calling, and she is foolish to worry over why the graduate student in his running shoes has come with a poster in the early afternoon. ("All that formality of may-I-come? or hope-we're-not-disturbing-you is for Westerners," the immigrants joke among themselves. She has heard it once already this afternoon from Mrs. Thapar. "We may have minted a bit of money in this country, but that doesn't mean we've let ourselves become Americans. You can see we've remained one hundred percent simple and *deshi* in our customs.") Vinita wants to remain *deshi* too, but being *deshi* and letting in this good-looking young man (a line darts across an imaginary page, enunciated in rotund Mauritian French and Vinita almost giggles: *Le jeune homme dont l'oeil est brillant, la peau brune, Le beau corps de vingt ans qui devrait aller nu* . . . and Vinita blushes again, more deeply), a young man who told her the first time they met, after a movie, that he'd been born in Calcutta but immigrated with his parents when he was just a toddler—letting him in might lead to disproportionate disaster.

"It is very kind of you, Mr. Khanna, to bring over Rooma Devi's poster," she says miserably. She has never heard of Rooma Devi. Rooma Devi cannot possibly be a ranking Odissi dancer. Yet Rooma Devi has succeeded in pounding thin whatever tranquility the promise of letter-writing had produced in Vinita.

"You remember my name, Mrs. Kumar?" It is not so much a question as an ecstatic exhalation. "But please call me Rajiv. Unless you want to call me Billoo, which was my pet name in India. Just don't call me Bill."

She is relieved that Rajiv Khanna is inside the condominium and that the period of indecision is over. He has somehow shut the front door behind him and has suspended his baseball cap on the smaller horse's ear.

"Would you like some authentic India-style tea?" she asks. It is the correct thing for an Indian hostess to do, even in New Jersey; to offer the guest something to drink, even if it's just a glass of water. "I am making it exactly like the *chai-wallahs*. I am boiling tea leaves in a mixture of milk, water and sugar, and throwing in pinches of cardamom, cloves, cinnamon, etcetera."

"I don't want you stuck in the kitchen," he laughs. "I want you to tell me stories about Calcutta. I was only three when Baba took the post-doctoral fellowship at Madison but I still remember what our alley smelled like in July and August." He laughs again, hyper and nervous. "Let's use teabags. You must take advantage of American shortcuts."

Rajiv Khanna stalks her into the living room, forcing her to take quicker steps than usual so his New Balances won't catch the thin, stiff leather edges of her Sholapuri slippers. She begins to see Sailen's Bloomingdale's decor—the pastel conversation pit made up of modular sofas, the patio-atrium corner defined by white wicker—the way a hard-up graduate student might, as opulent, tasteful. When Rajiv compliments her artistic touch, she swings back to smile at him, bashful but flattered.

An issue of *Technology Review* on an obviously new coffee table catches his eye, and he lingers in the conversation pit, one knee resting deeply on an ottoman. In that pose, he reminds her of marsh birds she had seen on vacations in rural Bengal. The image automatically makes her pitch her voice low. Her gestures now softly wary, so the bird will not fly off.

She slips off to the kitchenette to make tea. The work counter of butcher's block is a barrier against the unseemly jokes that fate might decide to try out on her. In fact, in the bluish-white fluorescent light that threatens to never burn out, her earlier fears now seem absurd.

"I miss the cultural events of Calcutta," she says chattily. "It's such a lively city. Always some theatrical program, some crafts exhibit, something that touches the heart." From the asylum of the kitchenette, she watches him flip through the pages of Sailen's magazine without actually reading. There's an archness to her posture, she knows. She can feel her body tauten the way it often had in college while Mother Stella sanitized the occasional salacious verse. *On n'est pas sérieux, quand on a dix-sept ans*, Rimbaud said, but now she thinks twenty-five is not a matronly age. Mrs. Mehra and Mrs. Thapar are at least ten years older than her. Sailen had specified to his parents that he wanted a youngish bride, one who could speak fluent English and who could—once he felt he could afford it—bear him two or three children. He has spoken to her of his dream of having a son play in Little League games. Hearing him dream aloud, she assumed that it wasn't so much a son that he wanted as to assimilate, to be a *pukka* American.

Rajiv Khanna ignores her comment. He sits astride the new coffee tables (she's distracted with worry that if the glass top breaks, it cannot be replaced; or more accurately, that if the table falls apart she'll have to confess, but confess to what?) and drums his thighs with his fingertips. The fingers are long, the fingers of a poet. No wonder he has not been absorbed by Sailen's *Technology Review*. She waits for him to make small talk, to keep up his part as charming guest.

"I can't believe I went through with it!" It's an outburst, and it confuses her. She busies herself with cups and saucers.

"I can't believe I had the courage!"

She steals a look at him, thankful for the cumulous clouds of steam from the boiling water. Courage for what? Instinctively, she smooths down the hair on her crown which she knows from experience turns frizzy in hot, humid weather. Girls should make the best of their looks. She's been taught this by the nuns at school and by her relatives for so long that prettying herself has become a habit, not a vanity. Rajiv approaches her, his gait uneven, nervous; he is a potential invader of her kitchenette-fortress.

"I knew you were special the very first time I saw you. At the India Republic Day celebrations at the Khoranas'. I told myself this is it, this is the goddess of my dreams. I couldn't get you out of my mind."

Vinita finishes steeping two Twining teabags in a teapot before responding to the young visitor's outburst. She is not as shocked as she had expected to be. Yes, she has rehearsed moments like this; she has put herself on the television screen, in the roles of afternoon wives taken in passion. Not as shocked as she *should* have been, she worries. A warmth (from Rajiv's compliment? from anxiety? the kettle's steam?) swirls just under her glycerine-and-rose-watered skin. She concentrates on making tea; the brew must be just the right amber color. But tea-making in New Jersey is no challenge. She plucks and dunks each bag repeatedly by its frail string. You give up a little taste, but you grab a little convenience cleaning up. The new world forces you to know what you really want.

He barks again. "You haven't discouraged me."

She shrinks behind the counter. He shakes an accusatory index finger. She draws the loose end of her sari over her right shoulder so that her arms, her silk-bloused breasts and bare midriff are swathed. But the sari was bought at the Sari Palace on Lexington, and her breasts seem to her to loom and soar, through the Japanese chiffon. The young man has turned her into a siren.

"I don't know what you mean." She wants to sound stuffy, but it comes out, she knows, innocent, simpering.

"You should have thrown me out minutes ago. You could have refused to let me in. I know you Indian girls. You could have taken the poster and slammed the door in my face. But you didn't!"

He is a madman. It's true; he *is* a madman, but she is no siren. She repeats this to herself, a litany against calamity. Because of his windbreaker and his running shoes she had assumed he was just another American, no one to convert her into a crazy emblem. She had assumed that he was the looter of American culture, not hers, and she had envied the looting. Her own transition was slow and wheezing.

"You offered to make tea instead." He sounds triumphant.

"It was the least I could offer a guest," she retorts. "I haven't lost all my manners because I've moved to a new country. I know some Americans won't even give you a glass of water when you drop in."

He is not listening. He blabs, high-pitched angry words undulating from his fleshy lips. Love, it would appear, torments Rajiv. The face, which she had initially considered symmetrical, now devastates her from across the butcher's block counter, the features harsh, moody. His New Balance shoes are anachronistic; he is a lover from the turn-of-the-century novels of Sarat Chandra, the poems of Rimbaud—*Oh! quel Rêve les a saisies . . . un rêve inouï des Asies, Des Khenghavars ou des Sions?*—unmoored by passion. One long-lashed furtive glance from the woman next door, the servant girl, the movie star, and the hero's calamitous fate is sealed. But this is America, she insists. There is no place for feelings here! We are both a new breed, testing new feelings in new battlegrounds. We must give in to the old world's curb.

"Let's be civilized," she pleads, by which she means, let's be modern and Indian. "Take your cup, and let's sit in the patio. My husband will be here any minute and he'd be so disappointed if you left without seeing him. He thinks you're a brilliant boy." She's pleased at her own diplomacy. She has nipped passion before it can come to full fury, she has flattered his intelligence and she has elevated herself to the role of older sister or youngish aunt.

"Confess!" he demands. "I must mean something special to you. Otherwise you wouldn't have tolerated me this long. You'd have called Mr. Kumar or the police."

"I think you are unwell," she ventures. She hates him for considering her lascivious. She hates herself for not having thought of calling her husband. But what could she have said over the phone to a dark-suited man in an office cubicle concentrating hard on a computer terminal? Please come home and protect me from that Khanna boy who fancies he's in love with me?

He lunges at her. Suddenly the kitchenette counter seems a frail barrier. Tea spurts into a pretty saucer and stains the butcher's block. She has no time to tear off squares of paper towel and wipe up the spill. His right arm snakes toward her, reaches up through the chiffon sari; the snake's jaws, closing on a breast, scratch her hand instead.

"Madman!" she screams. Her side, her breast, her hand, all burn with shame. The snake's jaws have found the breast. She is paralyzed.

"You have no right to play with my feelings, Vinita! Confess at once!"

The situation is absolutely preposterous. She has been taught by Mother Stella and by her parents how to deal with revolutions. She can disarm an emaciated Communist pointing a pipe-gun at her pet chihuahua. She can drive her father's new Hindustan Ambassador and she's beginning to drive on weekends to local shopping malls. But banal calamities, the mad passions of a maladjusted failed American make her shudder.

Rajiv lets go. He picks up his cup and saucer and flounces off to the patio. She watches him curl up on the wicker love seat, his New Balance shoes polluting the new cushions with street germs. He admires Sailen's careful grouping of rare orchids with all the confidence of an invited guest. All but one of the orchids are in their prime this afternoon, and their thick petals glow in the odd New Jersey light. Her breast tingles. It feels warm; it feels recently caressed. She leans her forehead against the fake Ionic column that marks off the alcove for the refrigerator, and wonders if the torment that the madman in her atrium feels is the same torment she too would have suffered if she had the courage to fall in love.

At seven-twenty, Sailen comes home. Tonight he has brought Vinod Mehra and Kailash Kapoor with him. They go to the same fitness club after work. Rajiv Khanna left soon after finishing his cup of tea, so Vinita has had time to bathe at five-thirty as usual (she maintains the Indian habit of bathing twice a day), to put on a purple silk sari that she knows looks quite seductive on her, dress her long hair elaborately with silver pins and cook dinner. The dinner includes six courses, not counting the bottled pickles and the store-bought pie for dessert. Cooking a fancy meal has been her self-acknowledged expiation, though in her heart she is sure (why shouldn't she be sure?) that she has committed no transgression. Now seeing the unexpected guests, she is relieved that their visit coincides with the night of her extra effort. What if she had made nothing but *dal*, rice and a vegetable curry? Rumors about Sailen Kumar's bride starving Sailen Kumar would have started to swirl through highrises in Brooklyn and Rego Park.

The men congregate in the atrium. It is quite obviously Sailen's pride and joy; therefore, by extension, it is Vinita's pride and joy, too. She watches him show off his newest acquisitions in plants and flowers. In India, where the gardener and his grandson had taken care of such things, she had thought of blossoms only in terms of interior decoration, how they look against a background of new pink silk drapes, for instance. Now she has to view them differently, as though selecting them at the florist's, nursing them through the winter in overheated rooms and pruning them to look their most gorgeous is self-expression. In fact, she has heard Sailen justify his choice of buying a condominium in New Jersey instead of across the river where the action is by pointing at the atrium. You couldn't afford that in Manhattan, no sir. Unless you were a millionaire. Of course, she knows that Sailen intends to be a millionaire, as do his close friends, especially Vinod Mehra. Everybody in the Indian community knows that Vinod Mehra is likely to reach his goal before he is fifty. He plays the stock market better than most professional brokers. Everybody respects him for being a money wizard.

She reminds her husband to fix their guests drinks—"I am knowing so little about shaking cocktails and pouring jiggers, I'm afraid," she apologizes with her infectious laugh—and runs between kitchenette and patio with spiced cashews and deep-fried tidbits like vegetable pakoras. It is obvious that the men find her seductive, charming and inviolable. They alternate between being deferential and being flirtatious. They plague her with questions about local politics in India. They tease her about being a spoiled, rich girl and therefore, a novice cook who makes pakoras and samosas. They beg her to sing them a Tagore song (but my

harmonium hasn't arrived yet!) because it's already gotten around (from that nice Khanna boy who studies at
Columbia, a bright boy, says Sailen) that she must be
a talented singer. She is ecstatic; she serves the men
and manipulates them with her youth and her beauty
and her unmaskable charm. She has no idea that she is
on the verge of hysteria. She has no idea.

That night in bed, for the first time since she has left
Calcutta, she is bothered by insomnia. Within reach,
but not touching her, Sailen sleeps on his stomach. He
is breathing through his mouth. She imagines his fleshy
lips; they flap like rubber tires. He is a good man, and
one day he will be a millionaire. He has never, not
once, by gesture or word, made her feel that she is
anything but the queen of his heart.

Why then is she moved by an irresistible force to
steal out of his bed in the haven of his expensive condominium, and run off into the alien American night
where only shame and disaster can await her?

The Imaginary
Assassin

I was born in Yuba City, California, in July—the month of *Sravan* by my grandfather's calendar—of 1960. Grandfather had first come to the Valley at age thirteen to visit relatives. The plan had been for Grandfather to slip into the illegal aliens' underground at the end of the visit, make a fortune, then bring in the rest of his family. In those days work with Sikh farmers wasn't hard to find. Many had started out just that way, as robust illegals on the run, and made fortunes in the Valley. Some claimed that they had had to marry off daughters to rich, ugly men in big cities like Amritsar and Delhi in order to pay the one-way fare to Los Angeles. But all such sacrifices had paid off, and in time they'd been able to bring over these daughters too, and *their* families.

California was paradise to starving men from dusty Ludhiana villages. But what good was access to paradise if you weren't happy? The first time around, California had made Grandfather homesick.

All the Sikhs in America, Grandfather'd complained,

were knock-kneed and weakly. They'd lost their *dum*, their zest, as soon as they'd landed overseas.

This was not at all true, of course. Many of our people in the Valley got into scuffles with local youths and with the police. We gave more than we got, and Sikh pride remained intact. But Grandfather as a teenager must have been stubborn as well as lonely. He drove himself out of paradise by getting picked up for shoplifting and did not return to live here until November of 1948, a month after a madman shot Mahatma Gandhi, the bony man in loincloth who delivered India from the British.

Some scandal surrounded Grandfather's second coming to the Valley. In our ancestral village in Ludhiana, which Grandfather had left as a young man to find happiness in Sind, all the men seem to have been highspirited. Grandfather's youngest uncle, younger than him by three years at least, had been jailed for spitting at a British soldier in 1926. My mother's older brother had fallen in love with a brigand's daughter and been slain by police bullets in a millet field. Incest, blasphemy, misadventure: in a small, dark guest room with papered walls, Grandfather sat cross-legged on the bed and initiated me into the family's marvelous prodigality.

I came to hate my parents. The shabby diligence of our immigrant lives in Yuba City shamed the romantic in me.

I was a headachy, bookish boy, a collector of foreign coins from visiting uncles who'd worked in Africa, Malaya, England and Germany. I was a gatherer and embellisher of nostalgic family gossip. Other California

kids had their rock stars to make life bearable; I had
my great-uncle the spitter and my uncle the foolhardy
lover. My younger sister, Manorma, inherited all the
Singh family's high spirits. She lives in Canada now,
organizes farm workers' unions in British Columbia and
has twice been arrested by Mounties. I was the good
student, the one destined (Father hoped) to break with
the Singh tradition of working the soil. He had dreams
and schemes invested in my getting good grades and
going on to Cal Tech for aerospace engineering. Father
counted on good grades, initiative and a neat appearance more than I did. Father studied the names of
scholarship winners. Yee, Wang, Yamamota: neat to a
fault, I would have to agree. Why did I harbor a secret
fascination with a different kind of immigrant, Sirhan B.
Sirhan? Can madmen, tuned in to God, derail our
ordinary destinies?

It was Grandfather, the teller of old-country tales at
dusk, who asked such questions. His tales were full of
spectacular coincidences and miracles. The death rattle
of a dutiful son could deafen a mother five hundred
miles away. Headless ghosts, eager to decapitate, could
hide in trees along dark country lanes.

One night when I was about nine or ten, Grandfather
told me a remarkable story. We had the little house
nearly to ourselves. Mother was out that night. She was
at the temple for a meeting of the temple's executive
committee. Manorma was sleeping over at Amrita Dug-
gal's, a slow girl with oily braids, with whom she would
quarrel in another three weeks. Father was out with
Uncle Pritam, having a bit of fun and forbidden whis-
key. Father was dismissed by the Sikh community as a
big-hearted man who'd never get rich. Money and manly

honor: these were the only virtues for our people. Father dreamed of wealth and virility too, and he had dozens of rags-to-riches schemes that got their start over scotch in Uncle Pritam's den. At heart Father was a merchant, an exporter and importer of other men's talents, not a farmer. His most recent project had been the printing of mail-order bride catalogs for Ludhiana women. We still had two hundred catalogs in our basement. I'm not against the bringing in of hardy, grateful peasant women. Manorma, with her high spirits and her shrill union-worker's voice, is no more likely to make a Yuba City Sikh happy than an illiterate, slow, Ludhiana girl. And the project might have made Father some money. But Mother made him fold his "Mutual Happiness, Inc." firm when fifteen American males, one from as far away as Scottsdale, Arizona, mailed in their subscriptions.

"Have you no shame?" Mother screamed. "You want to sell girls to *them* now?" She threatened to call the Bureau of Immigration and Naturalization with an anonymous tip.

That night Father was at Uncle Pritam's to talk over a new scheme, something more in the line of show biz. A new man from Varanasi was travelling from Valley town to Valley town and being put up by local Sikh and Hindu families. The man was charismatic, our people said. He was a holy man with special gifts. He would sleep on beds of nails in high school auditoria and church basements if the money from ticket sales were given to orphanages in India. The future of the world, the man believed, would be decided by embittered orphans. Father was eager to back the holy man and move Indian culture out of basketball courts and Unitarian basements. But this was in the late sixties when holy men from India were no longer a novelty.

Grandfather and I would have had the house all to ourselves if it hadn't been for a houseguest who slept in a cot in the basement. He was a slender young man in a cheap new suit. He must have been a progressive Sikh, because he wore no turban and his hair had a jagged, raw, freshly chopped-off look to it. He stayed in the basement all day, even ate his meals off a tray down there. Now and then we heard his ghostly footsteps as he paced the basement in new sturdy shoes with two-inch heels.

The night was warm and very windy. The winds came off the orchards with a mess of leaves and twigs. I could hear the cackle and swish of windblown headless ghosts. It was the kind of night when even a nine-year-old American boy with good grades can confess his fear of gods and unholy spirits.

Grandfather was in bed, sucking on a pinch of powdered tobacco leaf, when I came into the room. A forty-watt bulb in a broken wall fixture made the room seem dreary.

"Tell me a new ghost story," I begged.

He offered me the flat tin of powdered tobacco. I squeezed a large, gritty pinchful and dropped it on my tongue. He slipped the tin under his pillow and said, "Not a ghost story. I'll tell you a true story. I'll tell you why I had to come back to America to live."

"You *had* to? You mean someone forced you?"

"Yes," Grandfather said. "I killed a man in Delhi. I killed Mahatma Gandhi."

I didn't know what to do with this boastful confession. It wasn't true. Grandfather hadn't killed Mahatma

Gandhi. A Hindu fanatic had, at a public prayer meeting on October 2, 1948. The fanatic had been caught
and hanged. How could Grandfather lie to me about
verifiable history?

But Grandfather had an odd, zealous look in his good
eye—the other was creamy with cataracts—and asked
me to sit on the bed. He said, "Gurcharan, I'm going
to tell you what happened. This time it is not a story."

I said nothing. I pushed the quilt to one side, so I
could stretch out my legs without getting the sheets
dirty. Mother worked hard all day in a canning factory
and I didn't want to upset her about extra laundry.
Downstairs I could hear our unsocial houseguest pace
the unfinished basement floor. The warm, moist winds
had made us too restless.

This is the tale that Grandfather told me in a mixture
of Punjabi and English.

"In 1947, long before you, my little friend, were in
your mother's belly, a tall Englishman named Lord
Mountbatten and Mahatma Gandhi sat down to a lunch
of dalchapati. There were no knives and forks, and so
Gandhi was teaching Mountbatten to eat Indian-style,
with the fingers. Gandhi was flicking his tongue against
the sides of his fingers, against the fingertips, and saying, 'See, Your Excellency, this way, the lentil doesn't
drip.' The Englishman was not liking to eat with the
fingers and to get his nails messy. He was not liking
Indian peasant food. He was probably thinking, Indian
curries in silver bowls in the Nehru dining room, now
that is quite another story! But being a diplomat and a
gentleman, Mountbatten changed the subject from in-
edible food to politics. He said, 'Mr. Gandhi, how can

you expect His Majesty to give you national independence when civil war is about to break out between you Hindus and the Muslims?' But Gandhi had his answer ready. He said, 'God will guide the King, don't worry. But if I don't show you how to eat without cutlery, Your Excellency, you will go today with hunger pains in your belly.' Then Gandhi did what we do with chapatis on our plates. He held his chapati down with the heel of his right hand and with a quick flick of the fingers, tore off a biteable piece. 'Here, Your Excellency,' Gandhi explained. 'This bit I'm holding for you to see is Pakistan for the Muslims. The rest of the chapati on my plate, that's India for us Hindus. You are seeing, milord, how simple the question of sovereignty is?' That's how we got rid of the Muslims and the British quick-quick. A coarse wheat chapati in a peasant's hand gave us liberty.

"But liberty became a sad and bloody gift to us Hindus and Sikhs who lived in the bit of land that His Majesty King George gave away to the Muslims. The Muslims snatched, torched, spoiled. It is the way of human nature; I am not blaming Muslims. But Gandhi, the spiritual leader, what did he understand about evil and sin? A man with his head in the clouds does not see the shit pile at his feet.

"Men in uniforms put us refugees on trains. I was put on a train for Delhi. Delhi was everybody's first choice. In my compartment refugees crouched on seats, bunks, floor spaces, even on luggage racks, like monkeys. A pretty city-woman in a muddy silk *kameez* dozed on a cardboard suitcase so near me that I had to sit pigeon-toed all night. A wide red scar bled down her forehead. Dagger nicks marred the creamy brown skin of her arms and midriff. Oh, how heedless Mahatma Gandhi had been with our lives!

"Sometime deep in the night, the woman put both her hands on my thighs. I tautened my muscles. We were a trainful of insomniacs. Everybody could see everything. Refugees have no privacy. She laughed. She moved her fingers this way and that, and I twisted my knees out of her reach. She was quite demented, you see, thinking I was her husband who must have been killed. We were decent men and women thrown into indecent situations by a dalchapati-eating Gandhi. I admired her boldness at the same time that I was embarrassed by it.

"The woman touched me again. She prodded me on the knee. This time her fingers were wifely, tender, provocative. In that train of misery, she wanted conjugal sex. I felt lust swell as I tucked my feet under me on the seat. Ill-bred men were watching and making encouraging noises.

"She got off at dawn at a village, but her scar, her cruel, sleepless eyes, her lecherous touch, she left these behind to disconcert me. My own wife was dead. This woman was no better off. Gandhi had hurt our women. The man who could sleep between virgins and feel no throb of virility had despoiled the women of our country. Gandhi was the enemy of women. And so, Gandhi, the Mahatma, the Great Soul, became my enemy.

"When I got to Delhi, right away I set about to assassinate that man. I could think of nothing else. My body was made of stone; it suffered no hunger, no sun and rain. I'd need a weapon, and I'd need safe passage after the event. I saw myself raiding police depots and armories. I hoarded soda bottles to hurl into Gandhi's face. I held a gardener's job for a whole week so I could steal a hatchet. I mailed an aerogramme to your father. 'Sponsor my immigration,' I wrote him. 'I'll be in need of paradise any day.' Nights I dreamed of hacking the Mahatma to bits. Hindu saviors have dry, stringy bodies, the bodies of men who fast excessively. I was afraid the blunt blade of my hatchet wouldn't cut through Gandhi's armored flesh. He should have had the soft, lubricated flesh of politicians and business-men. The purity of my vengeance made me delirious. I read signs in shooting stars. The stars were women with accusatory faces.

"Months passed. My delirium kept me from holding regular jobs. Other refugees from West Punjab, ex-farmers like me, made new lives for themselves in new, desperate cities. They became itinerant cooks with stoves on wheels, they became washermen, taxi drivers, bus conductors. I couldn't settle down until I had killed. In my mind, Gandhi the celibate was the biggest rapist in history. I slept on sidewalks. I begged. I dreamed of public execution if safe passage to California failed.

"On October 2, Gandhi was to lead a public prayer meeting. October is a fine, cool month in Delhi, so the organizers expected millions to come out and pray. Gandhi was a genuine hero, a stooped little peasant like us in loincloth, who had driven King George away. But this time there were nasty rumors. We heard that even Gandhi clapped his hands over his ears because widows moaned too loudly under his balcony. They said that Gandhi knew about assassins in alleys. They said even a savior has his bitter moments and his dreams of fast-ing to death.

"The day of the prayer meeting, I tied the stolen

hatchet to my chest, slipped a loose *khadi kurta* over it, and followed the crowds. Worshippers choked the streets and lanes. Gandhians with "volunteer" arm bands guided us toward the garden where the prayer meeting was to be held. The Gandhians were ecstatic. They counted and recounted heads. But the policemen were sullen. They patrolled the boulevards in sweaty boots and pinned Gandhians against tree trunks to give them random bodychecks.

"I didn't care. I wasn't afraid. Many in our family are subject to nervous disorders. Euphoria kept me from all anxiety and pain. How often in life is our duty made so clear? How often is a man given the opportunity to avenge mass murder and rape?

"The Gandhians were slack-muscled. I kept my head down and pushed forward toward the garden. The Gandhians gave way. The police were watchful. But no hand jerked me out of line—truly God protects the saint—no baton fell on my head.

"Gandhi made us wait a while in the garden. The more important Gandhians stood in straggly rows on a platform. They were mill owners and politicians, the true beneficiaries of national independence. The rest of us gathered on grassy stretches, or climbed weak-limbed trees. One lady-Gandhian fell off a low branch and two policemen carried her away.

"Finally Gandhi came out of a building. Everyone started chanting, 'Raghupati Ravana'; it was Gandhi's special hymn. I did too, and my voice sounded loud and passionate. Gandhi looked pleased. He was a small, skinny man in a clean white loincloth, and he looked very pleased with us as he made his way to the platform in his bowlegged gait. Two very plain-faced girls held him by his elbows. They were his virgin bodyguards. They forced him into a brisker pace. When Gandhians reached for their savior, the girls swatted them gently away.

"I put out my assassin's hand. My fingertips touched sun-wrinkled flesh. Gandhians pushed me from behind, the girls took fast, mincing steps, and I lost my grip on the Mahatma. But he turned around, and I swear he smiled. 'Raghupati Ravana Raja Ram,' Gandhi chanted. 'Patita Pavana Sita Ram,' I finished, elated. This time Gandhi stopped. He shrank from the delirium in my eyes. But I reached out. We touched. I grabbed his dark, coarse, peasant flesh. These hands held the Mahatma's body. I pressed the Mahatma against my chest.

"A howl came out of him when he felt the hatchet. He scraped my *kurta* with his nails. He struggled, he meant to push me away but it looked like a brotherly embrace. No Gandhian would have guessed that even a savior might be unready for violent death. But death came to him all right, death came while he was slumped in my embrace. Bullets tore up Gandhi's skinny body. The body collapsed in my arms, it was a sad bloody mess.

" 'Ram, Ram,' we prayed for the Mahatma.

"A corpse, even a savior's corpse, jerks and stiffens in demeaning ways.

"Now comes the confusing part. The Mahatma died in my arms but it was not me that the police arrested that day. I killed the Mahatma out of delirious hate, but it was a slim, fair Hindu fanatic from Maharashtra that they arrested instead.

"I left Delhi for Bombay that night. There was talk of accomplices, of extremist Hindu parties with terrorist cells. From Bombay I fled to Liverpool, signing on as a lascar on a cargo boat. From Liverpool, I wrote your father and he sent me dollars for a boat ticket to New York and for a train to California. Who knows, if I had stayed in California the first time I came, I might have been a chartered accountant in a fancy tie and jacket. And poor Mahatma Gandhi like the rest of us might have lived out his life to embittered ripeness.''

At the end of the story, Grandfather straightened up against the headboard of the bed and recited lines from an English poem:

> For the world, which seems
> To lie before us like a land of dreams,
> So various, so beautiful, so new
> Hath really neither joy, nor love, nor light
> Nor certitude, nor peace, nor help for pain;
> And we are here as on a darkling plain
> Swept with confused alarms of struggle and flight,
> Where ignorant armies clash by night.

A nine-year-old Californian, I hadn't heard of Matthew Arnold. And I didn't know until much later that it was Grandfather, not the great-uncle, who had spat on the British captain in 1926 and had been forced to memorize *Dover Beach* in jail. I think now of the despair of that English soldier as he tried to subdue schoolboys on a subcontinent where night armies were already on the march. At nine I knew only that an illiterate and senile man reciting a foreign poem was a wondrous feat.

So that was how one summer night Grandfather told me the fantastic story of Mahatma Gandhi and himself.

The Californian boys had their rock stars and their movie stars and their cute sexy girlfriends who went all the way. I had nothing. The family's prodigality expresses itself in slow, secretive ways. From that night began my hallucinations and nervous spells that kept me from that desired good and neat appearance and the aerospace scholarship to Pasadena.

Father's show biz scheme came to nothing, again. In a school auditorium in San Diego, the holy man lost his concentration and tore his chest on a strip of nails. Father wasn't American enough to grasp the fact that blood is better show biz than any yogic performance.

The slender houseguest with the raw, amateurish haircut was picked up by Yuba City police the only night he left our basement. They said he'd killed another Sikh in Toronto, Canada. I don't know how, or why, or when.

Courtly Vision

J AHANARA Begum stands behind a marble grille in her palace at Fatehpur-Sikri.

Count Barthelmy, an adventurer from beyond frozen oceans, crouches in a lust-darkened arbor. His chest—a tear-shaped fleck of rust—lifts away from the gray, flat trunk of a mango tree. He is swathed in the coarse, quaint clothes of his cool-weather country. Jacket, pantaloons, shawl, swell and cave in ardent pleats. He holds a peacock's feather to his lips. His face is colored an admonitory pink. The feather is dusty aqua, broken-spined. His white-gloved hand pillows a likeness of the Begum, painted on a grain of rice by Basawan, the prized court artist. Two red-eyed parrots gouge the patina of grass at the adventurer's feet; their buoyant, fluffy breasts caricature the breasts of Moghul virgins. The Count is posed full-front; the self-worshipful body of a man who has tamed thirteen rivers and seven seas. Dainty thighs bulge with wayward expectancy. The head twists savagely upward at an angle unreckoned except in death, anywhere but here. In profile the lone prismatic eye betrays the madman and insomniac.

On the terrace of Jahanara Begum's palace, a slave girl kneels; her forearms, starry with jewels, strain toward the fluted handle of a decanter. Two bored eunuchs squat on their fleshy haunches, awaiting their wine. Her simple subservience hints at malevolent dreams, of snake venom rubbed into wine cups or daggers concealed between young breasts, and the eunuchs are menaced, their faces pendulous with premonition.

In her capacious chamber the Begum waits, perhaps for death from the serving-girl, for ravishing, or merely the curtain of fire from the setting sun. The chamber is open on two sides, the desert breeze stiffens her veil into a gauzy disc. A wild peacock, its fanned-out feathers beaten back by the same breeze, cringes on the bit of marble floor visible behind her head. Around the Begum, retainers conduct their inefficient chores. One, her pursed navel bare, slackens her grip on a *morchal* of plumes; another stumbles, biceps clenched, under the burden of a gold hookah bowl studded with translucent rubies and emeralds; a third stoops, her back an eerie, writhing arc, to straighten a low table littered with cosmetics in jewelled pillboxes. The Begum is a tall, rigid figure as she stands behind a marble grille. From her fists, which she holds in front of her like tiny shields, sprouts a closed, upright lotus bloom. Her gaze slips upward, past the drunken gamblers on the roof-terraces, to the skyline where fugitive cranes pass behind a blue cloud.

Oh, beauteous and beguiling Begum, has your slave-girl apprised the Count of the consequences of a night of bliss?

Under Jahanara Begum's window, in a courtyard cooled with fountains into whose basin slaves have scattered rose petals, sit Fathers Aquaviva and Henriques, ingenuous Portuguese priests. They have dogged the emperor through inclement scenery. Now they pause in the emperor's famed, new capital, eyes closed, abstemious hands held like ledges over their brows to divert the sullen desert breeze. Their faces seem porous; the late afternoon has slipped through the skin and distended the chins and cheeks. Before their blank, radiant gazes, seven itinerant jugglers heap themselves into a shuddering pyramid. A courtier sits with the priests on a divan covered with brocaded silk. He too is blind to the courage of gymnasts. He is distracted by the wondrous paintings the priests have spread out on the arabesques of the rug at their feet. Mother and Child. Child and Mother. The Moghul courtier—child of Islam, ruler of Hindus—finds the motif repetitive. What comforting failure of the imagination these priests are offering. What precarious boundaries set on life's playful fecundity. He hears the Fathers murmur. They are devising stratagems on a minor scale. They want to trick the emperor into kissing Christ, who on each huge somber canvas is a bright, white, healthy baby. The giant figures seem to him simple and innocuous, not complicated and infuriating like the Hindu icons hidden in the hills. In the meantime his eyes draw comfort from the unclad angels who watch over the Madonna to protect her from heathens like him. Soft-fleshed, flying women. He will order the court artists to paint him a harem of winged women on a single poppy seed.

The emperor will not kiss Christ tonight. He is at the head of his army, riding a piebald horse out of his new walled city. He occupies the foreground of that agate-colored paper, a handsome young man in a sun-yellow *jama*. Under the *jama* his shoulders pulsate to the canny violent rhythm of his mount. Behind him in a thick choking diagonal stream follow his soldiers. They scramble and spill on the sandy terrain; spiky desert grass slashes their jaunty uniforms of muslin. Tiny, exhilarated profiles crowd the battlements. In the women's palace, tinier figures flit from patterned window grille, to grille. The citizens have begun to celebrate. Grandfathers leading children by the wrists are singing of the emperor's victories over invisible rebels. Shopkeepers, coy behind their taut paunches, give away their syrupy sweets. Even the mystics with their haggard, numinous faces have allowed themselves to be distracted by yet another parade.

So the confident emperor departs.

The Moghul evening into which he drags his men with the promise of unimaginable satisfactions is grayish gold with the late afternoon, winter light. It spills down the rims of stylized rocks that clog the high horizon. The light is charged with unusual excitement and it discovers the immense intimacy of darkness, the erotic shadowiness of the cave-deep arbor in which the Count crouches and waits. The foliage of the mango tree yields sudden, bountiful shapes. Excessive, unruly life—monkeys, serpents, herons, thieves naked to the waist—bloom and burgeon on its branches. The thieves, their torsos pushing through clusters of leaves, run rapacious fingers on their dagger blades.

They do not discern the Count. The Count does not overhear the priests. Adventurers all, they guard from each other the common courtesy of their subterfuge. They sniff the desert air and the air seems full of portents. In the remote horizon three guards impale three calm, emaciated men. Behind the low wall of a *namaz* platform, two courtiers quarrel, while a small boy sneaks up and unties their horses. A line of stealthy women prostrate themselves and pray at the doorway of a temple in a patch of browning foliage. Over all these details float three elegant whorls of cloud, whorls in the manner of Chinese painting, imitated diligently by men who long for rain.

The emperor leaves his capital, applauded by flatterers and loyal citizens. Just before riding off the tablet's edge into enemy territory, he twists back on his saddle and shouts a last-minute confidence to his favorite courtpainter. He is caught in reflective profile, the quarter-arc of his mustache suggests a man who had permitted his second thoughts to confirm his spontaneous judgments.

Give me total vision, commands the emperor. His voice hisses above the hoarse calls of the camels. *You, Basawan, who can paint my Begum on a grain of rice, see what you can do with the infinite vistas the size of my opened hand. Hide nothing from me, my cowanderer. Tell me how my new capital will fail, will turn to dust and these marbled terraces be home to jackals and infidels. Tell me who to fear and who to kill but tell it to me in a way that makes me smile. Transport me through dense fort walls and stone grilles and into the hearts of men.*

"Emperor on Horseback Leaves Walled City"
Painting on Paper, 24 cms x 25.8 cms
Painter Unknown. No superscription
c. 1584 A.D.
Lot No. SLM 4027-66
Est. Price $750

About the Author

Bharati Mukherjee was born in Calcutta and lived in Toronto and Montreal before moving to the United States. She attended college in India and earned her doctorate from the University of Iowa. She is the author of three novels and one other collection of short stories. She has taught creative writing at Columbia, NYU, and Queens College, and she currently holds a distinguished professorship at Berkeley. She and her husband, writer Clark Blaise, have two grown sons.

BHARATI

MUKHERJEE

"Superbly delineates the tensions and contradictions encountered by these (today's) new Americans... an unusual angle of vision on the immigrant dream..."

Boston Herald